"I WAS WONDERING IF YOU WERE GOING TO SHOW UP, MISTER FARGO . . ."

"Wondering or worrying?" Skye asked, stepping into the room.

"Wondering," she said, her eyes narrowing a fraction.

"Liar," he answered. She didn't reply, but she let the door close, and he took that as an invitation. He pulled the thin string at the frilly lace of her nightdress and the lace collar came open, down to the swell of her breasts.

"You take a lot for granted," she murmured.

"I never take a good-looking woman for granted," Fargo said, smiling as he reached out for her . . .

D1714154

THE TRAILSMAN 10

SLAVE
HUNTER

by
Jon Sharpe

A SIGNET BOOK
NEW AMERICAN LIBRARY
TIMES MIRROR

NAL BOOKS ARE AVAILABLE AT QUANTITY DISCOUNTS WHEN USED TO PROMOTE PRODUCTS OR SERVICES. FOR INFORMATION PLEASE WRITE TO PREMIUM MARKETING DIVISION, THE NEW AMERICAN LIBRARY, INC., 1633 BROADWAY, NEW YORK, NEW YORK 10019.

The first chapter of this book appeared in *Dead Man's Saddle*, the ninth volume in this series.

SIGNET TRADEMARK REG. U.S. PAT. OFF. AND FOREIGN COUNTRIES
REGISTERED TRADEMARK—MARCA REGISTRADA
HECHO EN CHICAGO, U.S.A.

SIGNET, SIGNET CLASSICS, MENTOR, PLUME, MERIDIAN AND NAL BOOKS are published by The New American Library, Inc., 1633 Broadway, New York, New York 10019

First Printing, April, 1982

1 2 3 4 5 6 7 8 9

PRINTED IN THE UNITED STATES OF AMERICA

The Trailsman

Beginnings . . . they bend the tree and they mark
the man. Skye Fargo was born when he was
eighteen. Terror was his midwife, vengeance his
first cry. Killing spawned Skye Fargo, ruthless,
cold-blooded murder. Out of the acrid smoke of
gunpowder still hanging in the air, he rose, cried
out a promise never forgotten.

The Trailsman, they began to call him all
across the West, searcher, scout, hunter, the man
who could see where others only looked, his
skills for hire but not his soul, the man who lived
each day to the fullest, yet trailed each
tomorrow. Skye Fargo, the Trailsman, the seeker
who could take the wildness of a land and the
wanting of a woman and make them his own.

The Kansas Territory,
just before statehood—
a divided land—
half free and half slave.

1

"Ah, shit," Fargo swore softly as he watched the scene unfold. He'd come out to relax in the warm afternoon sun, to sit under the tree and do nothing except enjoy the roast-beef sandwich he'd brought with him. And clear last night's bourbon out of his head. Just sit and relax, maybe snooze a little. But the spring wagon with the wooden dasher had come racing over the hill, four horsemen riding hell-for-leather after it. A girl held the reins of the wagon, driving furiously, and beside her, an elderly gray-haired black man hunched low in the seat.

"Shit," Fargo muttered again as he took another bite of his sandwich. Whatever it was, he wasn't interested, he told himself as he sat against the tree, utterly relaxed and unmoving.

The girl could drive, he noted; she held the racing wagon under control as it careened down the long, sloping hillside. He could see her better now, long brown hair streaming out behind her in the wind. The elderly gray-haired black man half-turned to cast a quick glance at the pursuers, who were closing fast. The wagon was halfway down the slope when the four riders spread out to box it in. Two raced past it to the horse and the other two hung back at the tail. One of the men reached out to seize the horse's cheek strap and the girl lashed out with the whip. The man let go of the bridle and veered away, and Fargo heard his curse of pain.

1

Fargo watched one of the two at the rear. A man wearing a beige shirt and whirling a lariat raced his horse closer to the girl and tossed the rope. The lariat sailed over the girl to come around her, pulling her arms to her sides as the man pulled it tight. He knew how to rope, Fargo noted. He'd spent time as a cowhand.

The girl tried to pull herself free, dropped the reins to yank at the rope, but the rider pulled hard and she toppled backward into the rear of the wagon. Fargo caught her cry of fury and pain, mostly fury. The front riders moved in again, took hold of the horse's bridle, and brought the wagon to a halt.

The four riders surrounded the wagon, and the one in the beige shirt reached inside and half-lifted, half-dragged the girl out, then took the lariat from around her. She promptly hit him in the face with her fist and tried to kick him in the groin. Fargo could hear her curses as she attacked, but two of the others grabbed her from behind. The tallest of the four, wearing a red kerchief with black polka-dots around his neck, backhanded the girl twice across the face. "Damn little hellcat," Fargo heard him swear.

The elderly black man in the wagon was sitting stiffly, one of the men holding a six-gun into his ribs. Two of the others seized the girl's ankles, lifted, and her legs came up, her skirt falling upward on her thighs to reveal long legs, tanned and nicely curved. One of the men ran his hand up along the inside of her thighs and Fargo heard his laughter over the girl's curses. She tried to twist her body, but she was held in a firm grip. His hand reached the place he wanted. "Hot damn," he cried out.

"Later," the tall one with the dotted red kerchief said sharply. "First things first, dammit." The two men let go of her ankles, the girl's legs dropped, and she steadied herself on her feet. One kept hold of her, twisting her arm behind her back, and the other took the

2

horse's bridle. "That tree over there," Fargo heard the red kerchief order, and they started toward him, leading the wagon and pushing the girl along.

Fargo let breath blow from his lips in another deep sigh. Damn, he grimaced. His would be the only damn tree on the hillside. All he wanted to do was relax some, he muttered under his breath. In the wagon, the elderly gray-haired black man's hands were being tied behind his back and a length of lariat was being formed into a noose.

Fargo took a bite of his sandwich, was slowly chewing it when they reached the tree. They approached from the side, intent on their business, not seeing him at first, as he stayed silent and unmoving. His eyes flicked to the girl as the man holding her halted. She had a tight-skinned face, a long nose, a wide mouth, and a dimpled chin. Hazel eyes looked out from beneath thin brows, a face that made its own kind of prettiness out of a disparate set of features.

The red kerchief pointed to a tree branch and one of the others stepped forward, tossed the end of the noose over it, frowned in surprise as he saw the tall figure sitting almost directly under it. "Henson, look here," he called. "We got company." All eyes turned to him and Fargo saw the man called Henson step forward.

"Git," the man barked.

The long, outstretched figure didn't move, and Henson stared into lake-blue eyes as the black-haired man slowly took another bite of his sandwich. "I'm eating," Fargo said casually.

"Screw that. Go eat someplace else," Henson snapped. Fargo continued chewing. "You hear me?" the man growled.

Fargo swallowed. "I never talk with my mouth full," he said. "I was here first. Besides, this is the only tree around here."

3

One of the others cut in, nervousness in his voice. "Boss, we better get on with it. Tracy could be on his way now," he said.

Henson turned to him, his mouth tight. "All right, string him up," he ordered, returned his eyes to the long form under the tree. "You want to watch? You just keep eating and stay there," he ordered.

Fargo saw them yank the elderly black man to his feet in the spring wagon, slip the noose around his neck, start to tighten it.

"No, you rotten bastards," he heard the girl scream. She tried to rush to the wagon, but the man holding her arm just twisted as she gasped in pain. She turned her eyes on Fargo, pain in her hazel orbs. "You just going to sit there and watch?" she asked, and he saw anger and despair darken her eyes. "What kind of a man are you?" she flung at him. "*Do* something."

Fargo took a last swallow of his sandwich, let a long sigh escape him, eyed the girl. There was a terrible despair wrapped inside the fury of her accusing glare. He let his eyes go to the man called Henson. "Why are you so all-fired bent on hanging that man?" he asked mildly.

"None of your goddamn business," Henson spit back. "You just sit and watch or we'll make it a double hanging."

The man fixing the noose jumped down from the wagon. "All set," he said.

"No," the girl screamed out. "You can't. No."

Henson smirked up at the gray-haired black man who now stood in the wagon, the noose around his neck. "Ain't you gonna beg a little, blackie?" he sneered.

Fargo watched the old man's eyes meet Henson's sneer. In the lined, old face there was no pleading, not even anger, only a deep, immovable dignity.

"Finish it," Henson barked angrily.

4

One of the others raised his hand, brought it down hard on the horse's rump. The horse reared, bolted forward with the wagon, and the shot rang out at precisely the same instant. The rope parted as the bullet tore it in two. The old black man fell to his knees inside the wagon as it sped off. The others turned to stare at the black-haired man under the tree. He hadn't moved, they saw, the sandwich still in his left hand. His right hand was still at his side, but now the big Colt .45 was in it.

"You son of a bitch!" Henson frowned in astonishment. "Take him," he ordered. The others started toward the figure against the tree and Fargo raised the Colt a fraction.

"Somebody will get dead quick," he said quietly, but his voice was made of cold steel. The men halted, glanced at Henson. "It could be you," Fargo said to the man, and now the Colt was raised a fraction more. "I asked you a question. Now I'd like an answer," he said. "Why were you trying to hang that man?"

"And I said none of your goddamn business," Henson threw back.

"Because Joseph Todd ran away from them," Fargo heard the girl answer. "From being one of their boss's slaves."

Fargo motioned with the Colt. "Let go of her," he said, and the man holding her arm stepped back, released his grip. Out of the corner of his eyes, the big black-haired man saw the man at his left dip his knees a fraction, knew what the movement meant. The Colt fired as the man reached for his gun, his hand not more than halfway to the holster. The shot slammed into his abdomen and the figure doubled over, seemed to be pulled backward by invisible strings, then pitched forward, both hands clutching his midsection.

"Aaaagh . . . oh, Jesus, help me," the man cried out.

Henson and the other two stared at the big man under

5

the tree. He still hadn't moved, his long legs stretched out in complete relaxation. The hazel-eyed girl's stare held on him, her wide mouth open. The wounded man groaned again, and red rivulets seeped out between the fingers of his hands as they clutched his abdomen.

"He needs Doc Sweeney bad," one of the others said.

"Take him," Fargo said. "I figure there'll be no more stupid moves again, right?"

Two of the others bent down and lifted the limp form, draped it across one of the horses. Henson, one hand on his saddle horn, stared at the man still lounging beneath the tree.

"Who the hell are you, mister?" he asked. "One of her kind?"

"What's her kind?" Fargo asked mildly.

"Free-staters. John Brown's dirty rabble," Henson said.

"I never followed John Brown," the girl snapped. "He means anyone who's against slavery," she said to Fargo.

Henson swung onto his horse as the others started off with the wounded man. "Well, are you, mister?" he pressed.

"I never could see one man owning another," Fargo said. "But I'm no part of anything."

"Just a goddamn busybody, eh?" the man growled.

"Just someone trying to finish a sandwich," Fargo said. "Now ride, before I lose my temper, then the doc will have another customer."

The man wheeled his horse, glared back at Fargo. "Tell you one thing, mister. That blackie's as good as dead and so are you," he said. He slapped the horse, galloped after the others, and Fargo shifted his glance into the distance where the wagon had come to a halt, returned his eyes to the girl. She was studying him, trying to see behind the rugged, handsome face. Fargo let his own glance take her in more fully now, the wide mouth nicely shaped, made for pleasant warmth though she

6

held it grimly. The disparate features somehow came together to form a thoroughly attractive face, he noted again. She held her slender body very straight, narrow hips, and under the shirt her breasts seemed long, filling out at the bottoms with a nice roundness.

"You come on very different, mister," she said thoughtfully. "I didn't think you were going to do anything."

"I kept hoping I wouldn't have to," Fargo said. "Better go get your wagon."

"I'll be back," she said, starting to walk away.

"Don't bother. I just want to relax," Fargo said, and pushed himself back against the tree trunk, slipped the Colt into its holster, and took another bite of the sandwich. "Damn," he murmured again as he finished chewing the last bite, closed his eyes, and enjoyed the shade of the tree. He didn't open them until he heard the sound of the wagon drawing to a halt.

The elderly black man climbed down, hands untied now, and Fargo pushed himself to his feet as the man stretched his hand out to him. "May I know your name, sir?" he asked, his voice low and soft. "Mine, as you know, is Joseph Todd."

"Fargo, Skye Fargo," the big black-haired man said, taking the offered hand.

"I am in your debt, sir," Joseph Todd said.

"Forget it," Fargo said. He looked at the girl, his eyes questioning.

"I'm Amity Sawyer," she said, peered hard at him again, her eyes moving up and down the tall powerful frame. "You didn't look so big lying down," she said. A tiny frown came into her eyes. "Did you mean what you said to Henson, about not being a part of anything?" she asked.

"I did," Fargo answered with definiteness.

"Well, I'm afraid you're a part of something now," she said. "They'll be back looking for you, so I wouldn't

7

keep relaxing under that tree, even though you're some shot with that six-gun."

Fargo appraised her again. "Got any ideas?" he asked. "I'm not much on running."

"Come to my house with us. An explanation is in order and we can talk there," Amity Sawyer said.

"Don't they know where you live?" Fargo questioned.

"Of course they do, but they won't be taking Joseph out of my house, not yet, anyway. You have to appreciate the full picture to understand it. Please come with us?" she asked.

Fargo thought for a moment. He never liked knowing only a part of something, especially when it could affect his own neck. It was like knowing that a cougar attacked but not knowing when and how and why. "All right," he told her, and called the pinto from around the other side of the tree. Amity Sawyer's eyes widened as she saw the horse appear, the gleaming black forequarters with matching hindquarters and the sparkling white in between.

"An Ovaro," she murmured as Fargo swung onto the horse. "Magnificent." Her eyes went to Fargo, narrowed as she peered at him again. "No ordinary horse. No ordinary rider, I'm thinking," she murmured. She started the wagon rolling and Fargo swung the pinto alongside the driver's seat where Joseph Todd had climbed back to sit beside the girl, his hands folded in his lap.

"You can start explaining some along the way," Fargo said. "Who's this Tracy feller they seemed to want to avoid?"

"Sheriff Tracy. They saw Jimmy ride off and knew what I'd sent him to do," she said.

"Who's Jimmy?" Fargo asked.

"My little cousin. He's thirteen and he lives with me," Amity Sawyer said.

"Go on," Fargo said. "That's not much explaining so far."

"I am a runaway slave, Mr. Fargo," Joseph Todd said, investing the term with a special, almost prideful tone.

"You're not a slave, Joseph. You never were," the girl cut in angrily.

Fargo watched the elderly black man's rueful smile. "Meaning no disrespect, but Miss Amity doesn't like to face reality," he said. "I have belonged to Mr. Richard Thornbury for the past six months, one of his slaves, as completely as if I'd been one all my life."

"And I arranged to help Joseph escape," Amity said. "It would have worked perfectly, but Henson came back early. We ran into him as we pulled away from the back of the Thornbury place. He called the others and came after us."

"How do you come into this?" Fargo asked her.

The girl guided the wagon over a low hill and Fargo saw the big stand of box elders along a road. "Joseph Todd worked for my father for fifty years," Amity Sawyer said. "Worked, Fargo, not as a slave, as a free man drawing a free man's salary." She drove down the road, swung the wagon around a sharp curve, cast a sidelong glance at the big man riding beside her. "Are you aware of what's going on here in the Kansas Territory?" she asked.

"I might've heard some talk, but I don't pay much attention to talk," Fargo said.

"What are you doing here in the territory, Fargo?" the girl asked, and he saw Joseph Todd listening with quiet interest.

"I was following somebody, a lead, and it took me here. Turned out to be the wrong man," Fargo said.

"You're a lawman?" Amity asked.

"No," he said.

"A bounty hunter?"

9

"No. It was personal," he said.

Amity drove around a curve and the house was directly in front of them, sitting across the road like a giant bullfrog. A stable, weathered and with too many split planks in it, stood to one side. "Home, sweet home," the girl said with a trace of bitterness in her voice.

"I'll stable the wagon, Miss Amity," Joseph Todd said, and the girl leaped to the ground, landing lightly and gracefully on her feet.

Fargo tethered the pinto to a hitching post and followed her into the house, his sweeping glance taking in more details than most would see in an hour. Houses were like people, he'd always felt. The years left imprints. Some showed it more, some less. Some looked forward, others back. This house was a tired house, echoing better days in a hundred little ways, a cracked stairway banister, floorboards that needed resurfacing, a chipped mantel over the fireplace, good solid furniture frayed in too many places.

"Drink," the girl offered, opening a wooden cabinet against one wall. "I can use one."

"Bourbon," he said.

Joseph Todd returned and stood unobtrusively in the background for a moment, as she handed Fargo the drink, took a long pull on her own, and slid into one of the stuffed chairs. Fargo sat down across from her and watched her as she leaned back, her long breasts falling gracefully to the sides.

"How about pulling together what you've told me?" Fargo suggested. "It still doesn't fit anyplace."

"There's a terrible battle going on here in the Kansas Territory. This is a land divided between those who are slaveholders and those who are not, between those who favor slavery and those who hate it," Amity said. "It's tearing the territory apart. But those who favor slavery are ruthless, have more money, and are better organized."

"Where does the law stand?" Fargo asked.

Amity Sawyer uttered a harsh, bitter sound. "The law? The law's been changed so many times nobody knows what it means anymore. First there was the Missouri Compromise, then the Kansas-Nebraska Act, which made a mockery out of the Missouri Compromise, then the Dred Scott decision, and then the Lecompton Constitution, everything at cross-purposes, everything meaningless."

"Which really means that people do whatever they damn well please and the local law is whoever carries the most clout," Fargo said.

"Another bull's-eye for the man," Amity said bitterly.

"But that doesn't tell me how Joseph Todd became a slave?" Fargo said.

"My father died a year ago. I told Joseph to go north, that I'd help him get there. There is an organization that helps in that. But he wouldn't go," she said, casting a glance of loving disapproval at Joseph Todd.

"It wouldn't have been right to just leave Miss Amity and Jimmy here alone with all the problems she had facing her after Mr. Sawyer's passing," the man said.

"Joseph went to town without me one day six months ago. Henson and his men seized him on the way back and took him to the Thornbury place, and from then on, he was theirs. I went to Sheriff Tracy, but Richard Thornbury swore up and down that he'd always been theirs."

"It seems this Sheriff Tracy doesn't carry a lot of weight," Fargo thought aloud. "Why in hell did they worry about him showing up at all?"

"It's not as simple as that," Amity said. "Sheriff Tracy's not a bad man, not even weak. He's a confused man who hasn't any firm opinions of his own, so he's tried to

11

enforce a set of rules to keep some kind of order. No lynching is one of them. No raiding anyone's home to take a slave. No trying to free a slave."

"Which would put you on the wrong side there," Fargo said.

"I know that, but I sent Jimmy for the sheriff to stop a lynching," Amity said.

"He'd have been too late," Joseph Todd interjected. "But for you, I'd be swinging now, Mr. Fargo, and maybe Miss Amity'd be shot dead."

"You figure Henson would do that, too?" Fargo asked.

"Dead witnesses can't talk," the man said.

"This Richard Thornbury, he's that rotten an apple?" Fargo commented.

"He's a ruthless man as well as very smart and very smooth. He knows how to look the other way and let Henson do the actual dirty work," Amity said.

"It sounds to me like the sheriff's rules are broken pretty damn regularly," Fargo said.

"They are, but he tries, and I give him credit for that. It'd be total lawlessness without him here, the way it is in some other parts of the territory," Amity said.

Fargo's ears caught the sound of a horse approaching before the others did, and he glanced out the window, saw the young boy riding up alone.

"It's Jimmy," Joseph Todd said.

Fargo's eyes were on the door as the boy rushed in, brown curly hair, a round-cheeked face full of the breathlessness of youth. The boy's brown eyes lighted as he saw Joseph Todd, and his face broke into a happy grin.

"You made it, Joseph," he half-shouted. "You're safe."

"Thanks to this gentleman here, Jimmy," the man said, and the boy's glance went to the big black-haired man, instant respect coming into his young eyes.

"What happened with Sheriff Tracy, Jimmy?" Amity asked.

"I told him and he went out, took Ned with him," the boy said.

"Ned's his deputy," Amity explained.

"But we didn't come onto anything, so he went back and I came here," the boy said.

"Come on, I'll tell you all about it while I fix you something to eat," Joseph Todd said to the boy as they disappeared down a hallway.

Fargo looked at Amity Sawyer. "What happens now?" he asked.

"I must get Joseph to safety up north. You heard Henson's threat," she said.

"How do you figure to do that?" Fargo asked her.

"There are ways. We have an organization in the territory," she said.

"Your own underground railroad?" Fargo said. "I've heard about others."

"It's dangerous, and I'll have to make connections, have everything ready," she said. "Not many make it," she added grimly. "It'll be even harder with Henson waiting and watching. You'll be a lot of help, though."

Fargo's eyebrows lifted. "I'll be what?" he echoed.

"A lot of help," she repeated, the hazel eyes taking on a hint of haughty expectation. "You have to help us," she said.

"Why?" Fargo frowned.

She leveled a slightly smug look at him. "Henson threatened you, too. He said you were as good as dead, too," she returned.

Fargo's smile was slow, patience in it. "Sweetie, if you had a nickel for every sodbuster who's threatened me and was sorry he did, you'd be a damn rich woman," he said.

"But you can't just walk away now," Amity Sawyer

13

said, the color rising in her cheeks. "You must stay and help us."

"I did my piece," Fargo said coldly.

"And you think that's enough?" she flung back.

"I told you, I'm not part of anything. I've my own roads to travel. The name's Fargo, not Robin Hood," he told her.

He watched her lips bite down onto each other, and her hazel eyes held more than anger, a hint of despair inside their fury. She ran her tongue over her lips and he watched her searching for words to use as weapons. She was still groping for them when the window shattered with a crash of glass. Fargo whirled, bending at the knees, the Colt in his hand instantly, and his eyes saw the rock hit the floor, roll a few inches. He was at the window in one stride and heard the sound of a horse running away at full gallop. He caught a glimpse of the horse disappearing around the curve in the road, the rider pressed low and flat in the saddle. He muttered an oath as he slid the Colt back into the holster, turned to Amity.

She had picked up the rock and he saw the square little piece of paper attached to it with a rubber band. Amity pulled the little square of paper free, opened it. Her lips parted and Fargo heard the small gasp escape her. Staring down at the piece of paper, the color drained from her face, she stood transfixed.

Fargo reached out, took the little square of paper from her hands as she continued to stare at it, and he felt her tremble. He looked down at the paper, felt his own frown dig into his brow. There was only a drawing on it, a picture of a rifle, done in broad, crude lines. He looked up at Amity as she slowly turned to him and he saw shock mixed with fear in the hazel eyes. She moved her lips, but the words took a moment to form. "It's the sign," she said, her voice tight. "Oh, God, it's the sign."

"What sign?" Fargo queried, a hint of impatience coming into his voice.

"The sign of the slave hunter," she said. "It means Joseph has been marked."

"Who the hell is the slave hunter?" Fargo pressed.

"A one-man death squad," Amity said. "A hunter of runaway slaves. When the slave hunter is called in, it means death."

"You figure the Thornburys called him in?"

"Probably," Amity said.

Fargo frowned at her. "Probably?"

"Nobody ever knows who calls him in or if he decides on his own. There are others beside the Thornburys. There's an association of slaveholders. They work together."

"And nobody knows who this slave hunter is?" Fargo questioned.

15

"Nobody," Amity said.

"That can't be. How do they call him in?"

"I'm told that names are left at a drop somewhere. No one ever sees him or knows anything more until his mark appears," she said, looked down at the rifle on the slip of paper, slowly crushed the little square in her hand.

"Anybody ever get a look at him?" Fargo asked.

"Only from a distance, for a moment. He wears a black outfit, a black hat and a black mask," she said. "No runaway marked by the slave hunter has ever escaped alive. Some runaways, when they found out they were marked, ran back to slavery rather than be killed by the slave hunter."

"He's effective in more ways than one," Fargo thought aloud.

"Don't tell Joseph about this," Amity said. "His knowing won't help anything and maybe Joseph will be the first to escape the slave hunter." The hope in her words was undercut by the despair in her tone, and he watched her summon determination around herself like a cape.

"You figure to lay low for now?" he asked.

"No, I've got to move even more quickly. Joseph's only chance is to get to Illinois, to Peoria. He'll be safe there. I've got to contact the others at once," she said.

"The others who make up your underground railroad," Fargo commented, and she nodded.

"A band of people who believe together in what we're doing is right. We've a way, a system. We've gotten enough to safety," Amity said.

"But none marked by the slave hunter," Fargo said.

Her face grew tight for a moment. "No, we've failed there. But so has everyone else. We're not the only group helping runaways to find freedom. That's why you've got to help me get Joseph to safety, now more than ever," she said.

"I thought I answered that," Fargo said.

The hazel eyes grew angry instantly. "You can't just turn your back, dammit," Amity snapped.

"I wish you well, I honestly do, but I've my own trails to follow," he said. "I told you that."

She started to fling back words, halted as the sound of horses came from outside. Jimmy entered the room, excitement holding his smooth, young face. "It's Sheriff Tracy and Ned," he said, opening the door, and the two men appeared, entered the room. Amity nodded to the first man, her face unsmiling.

"Skye Fargo, this is Sheriff Sam Tracy, Deputy Ned Galloway," she introduced.

Fargo took in the two men. The sheriff had dark-gray eyes that seemed perpetually narrowed, a tall man, an angular frame with high-set shoulders and long arms. They could reach the Walker Colt at his hip pretty damn quickly, Fargo wagered silently. He had a face both lean and lined. The deputy, shorter, younger, dark-haired, tried to emulate his boss's probing eyes and only partially succeeded.

"Skye Fargo," the sheriff said, turning the name slowly on his tongue. "That could explain a lot of things," he added.

"Meaning what, Sam Tracy?" Amity asked sharply.

"I heard what happened," he answered, tossing the girl a glance, then looking back at Fargo. "Skye Fargo the Trailsman?" he asked.

Fargo nodded. "Some people call me that," he said.

"I've heard you never lose a trail or gunfight. I guess I believe it now," the sheriff said.

Fargo shrugged, aware that Amity's hazel eyes were boring into him. The sheriff turned his attention to the girl. "I'm glad it all ended the way it did," he said, "before I got into it."

"They tried to lynch Joseph. You ought to bring in that Henson, the Thornburys, too," Amity flared.

"I'm told you started it by running Joseph off their place," the sheriff said.

"He was a prisoner. They took him by force. You know that," Amity snapped.

"Knowing and proving's two different things. You know my rules, Amity. They're all I can do," the man said.

"They're not enough," she returned. "You sit in the middle and the slave hunter goes on killing."

Fargo saw the sheriff's face harden. "You and your friends feel one way, others around here feel different. They pay my salary, too. I'm not taking sides. I'm just trying to keep some law and do the best I can. Now you keep your Joseph Todd here. I don't want any more trouble," Sam Tracy told her. He turned his narrowed eyes on the big black-haired man. "I hope you aim to go your way peaceably, Fargo," he said. "I don't need anyone firing things up any more around here."

"That's what I figure to do," Fargo said amiably, watched the sheriff give Amity a curt nod and stride from the room, his deputy following on his heels. Fargo watched through the window as the two men mounted their horses and rode away. The sheriff's words hung in his thoughts for a moment. Advice, a warning, or something more, he wondered idly. One thing was plain: the sheriff didn't want outsiders around.

Fargo felt Amity's eyes on him, turned to her, and saw her studying him, moving up and down his big powerful frame. His smile was slow as he read her eyes. "It's about time. I was wondering about that," he said casually.

"You were wondering about what?" She frowned.

"Whether you ever looked at a man as a woman instead of some damn crusader," he answered.

A faint touch of color crept into her cheekbones. "Is that what I was doing, you think?" she returned.

"I don't think, I know," he said.

The hazel eyes refused admittance, but they made no denial, either. "It seems you've a reputation," she said.

"People talk." He half-shrugged.

"The Trailsman," she said, her lips pursing, and suddenly she was very female, interest and calculation obvious in her eyes. "You hire out, obviously, for money," she said.

"Sometimes," he conceded. "When I want, how I want."

"I'll hire you to get Joseph to safety," she said. "For pay."

Fargo let his eyes move around the room. "It doesn't seem to me you've a lot to spare, Amity Sawyer," he said, not ungently.

"I'll get the money," she snapped, and he caught the note of desperate determination in her voice. "We've a fund."

"Money won't mean anything," Fargo told her. "I've my own trails to follow. This isn't my fight."

"It will be one day," she threw back. "It's coming to that. Everybody will have to take a stand."

"Maybe. When that time comes, I'll be counted, one place or another, but not before," he answered.

"But you said you were against one man owning another," she countered, half-angry, half frustrated.

"I'm against a lot of things. I don't figure to fix them all," he said.

She turned from him, her lips biting down on each other, her long-waisted figure curving in a gentle bend, the long line of her breasts a lovely crescent.

He took her arm, turned her to him, and saw the

19

wetness in her eyes. She blinked it away at once. He edged down onto the sofa, pulled her with him. "There's more in it than the principle for you," he said.

She flung a quick glare at him. "That's enough. Believing in something is enough," she said.

"It is, but there's more with you," he insisted.

She folded her hands in her lap, looked down at them as she began to answer. "Years back, my pa was almost killed in a blizzard, the fierce ones we have out here. He'd gone out to try and round up some calves that had gotten out of the barn. He knew they were lost and confused and he wanted to save them. That's the kind of man he was. But his horse fell and he was hurt, helpless and freezing in the blizzard. It was Joseph who went out and found him and brought him back. He saved my pa's life and now I've a chance to repay that," she said.

"What if you can't?" he asked softly.

"I can try, with every last ounce of strength in me," she blazed back. "Joseph deserves that as a free man."

Fargo sat back and watched her send off waves of unvarnished honesty. She threw attractiveness at you in sudden moments, a toss of her head, a fleeting expression, a flash that made her face take on quicksilver loveliness. Damn, he swore inwardly. He was back under that damn tree trying to finish his sandwich again. She deserved help, but you could run yourself into the ground doing good deeds. He'd give her one more try and that'd be it, he thought, looked at her with annoyance.

"Maybe I can do something," he said, saw the hope flood into her face at once. It vanished as he went on. "I'll go visit the Thornburys," he said. "If they contacted the slave hunter, maybe I can get them to back off. Besides, I'd like to see a few things for myself."

"Think I'm making up stories, do you?" she flared.

"No, I didn't say that. I just want to see for myself,"

Fargo answered. "Sometimes a stranger carries more weight. By now I'm sure they've heard what happened. If they think I might be around, they could back away."

Amity sniffed disdainfully. "They won't pay you any mind," she said.

"It's worth a try," he insisted.

"Go on, do as you please," she said snappishly. Then, meeting his eyes she added, "You can stay the night here afterward, if you like," she said.

"Thanks," he said. "It'd be closer than hauling myself all the way to town."

"First room down the hall," she said. "I might be away when you get back, or asleep. I've wheels to set moving." She turned, started to walk away, and then halted, turned again, and came back to him, and her hazel eyes were full of warmth. "I'm sorry for digging so hard at you. I'm beholden to you for what you did today. I've no right to ask more," she said.

No performance, no guile, he realized, just the churning emotions inside her bursting forth and, with it, that sudden appealingness of her. He watched her hurry away, her long-waisted body moving with easy grace, a smooth stride that let her rear glide instead of bounce.

She disappeared down the hallway and Fargo saw Jimmy return. He'd stayed outside after Sam Tracy had left. The darkness was setting in fast, Fargo saw, and the boy halted before him.

"Joseph's fixed a bite to eat in the kitchen. He asked if you'd like something," Jimmy said.

"Lead the way," Fargo said, smiling, and followed the boy down the hallway to where an old stone kitchen opened up, a wooden table in the center, a stone hearth to one side, iron kettles on pegs in the wall. Joseph Todd had a chicken sliced on the table with some greens and scallions.

"Dig right in, please," Joseph said. "Care for a little sipping whiskey to wash it down?"

"Sounds fine," Fargo said. He saw Jimmy watching him, his young face filled with awe.

"How'd you learn to shoot like that, Mr. Fargo?" the boy asked. "Joseph told me all about it."

"Some of it comes with practice and some of it comes natural," Fargo said. "You live here all the time, Jimmy?"

"Yes, Pa Sawyer took me in when my folks died," the boy said. "Of course, Amity's been running things since he passed on."

Fargo let his eyes go to Joseph Todd. "She's had kind of a rough time, hasn't she, Joseph?" Fargo asked.

The old black man's face took on a quiet sadness. "There've been a few poor crop years and she put a good deal of her money into the Free State Association," he said. "That's a group who want to see Kansas become a free state. They use they money for Washington lawyers, for reaching important people there and for helping local groups all over."

"You mean hiring hands to help with the underground railroads and paying off local lawmen," Fargo added, and Joseph Todd half-smiled. "But you're not paying off Sam Tracy," Fargo said.

"No, not Sheriff Tracy, leastwise not the free-staters," Joseph said.

"Meaning maybe the slave-owners are?" Fargo said.

"Maybe," Joseph said. "The sheriff's a close man. No one knows what he thinks, really."

"Amity wants you to get out of here, you know," Fargo said. "What will she do here without you, Joseph?"

"I've told her to leave, too. She can come back again when all this is settled. It'll be another day then, another time," Joseph said.

"She's afraid the others will burn everything to the ground," Jimmy said.

"They can't burn the land," Joseph remarked. "That'll still be hers. She can start over. Staying here now is dangerous for her. Too many people know she's been backing the Free State Association. But Miss Amity's got a mind of her own."

Fargo pushed his chair back, finished the bourbon and a last bite of chicken, and stood up. The night was dark outside. "What's the best way to the Thornbury place?" he asked.

Joseph's face wrinkled in surprise. "Down the road, go right at the two pin oaks and take the trail that curves. You'll see the place when you come to it, big house it is," he said, and asked nothing further. Joseph Todd had lived long enough to know what questions were either too early or too late.

Fargo walked out to the pinto, Jimmy tagging along beside him, his eyes wide with admiration as they scanned the horse.

"Could I ride him sometime, Mr. Fargo?" he asked.

"I guess I'll be around long enough for that," Fargo said. "Tomorrow morning, maybe."

The boy nodded eagerly and Fargo swung onto the pinto, moved off at a trot. He thought he glimpsed a face with brown hair hung loose at one of the windows, but he wasn't certain and he took the road to the pin oaks, followed Joseph's direction.

It turned out to be a fair distance before he saw the lights of the house in the darkness, twinkling like distant fireflies. He swung behind two carriages that drove through the front gate of the Thornbury spread and slowed, his eyes taking in a dozen or more buckboards and carriages crowding the front driveway. The Thornburys were entertaining, in a big way, and he threaded

23

the pinto through the carriages to a hitching post along the side.

The house was white, big, with four columns fronting a wide portico, looked like a misplaced Southern mansion. A wide stream of light stretched out from the open front doors and Fargo glimpsed the white foyer and, beyond it, the big room with crystal chandeliers, crowded with women in fancy gowns and men in their dress-up gear. He stepped into the foyer when he saw Henson, to one side, the man's eyes widening in surprise.

"Damn, you got some nerve coming here," the man growled.

"Maybe," Fargo said quietly.

Henson started toward him, his hand half-reaching toward his holster, his face dark with anger, and he halted abruptly as he read the warning in the big man's blue-quartz eyes. Fargo saw one of the others who'd been at the attempted lynching standing to one side, apprehension in his face.

"Get out," Henson said.

"I'll let the Thornburys tell me that," Fargo said almost casually.

Henson's tongue flicked across his lips, indecision racing through his face. Fargo let his hand hang idly on the edge of his gun belt. "A man can get killed letting his temper get the best of his judgment," he remarked mildly.

"What is it, Henson," Fargo heard the voice ask, a soft, velvety voice, and his glance went past the man's figure to see the young woman approaching from the main room. He felt the instant surge of appreciation inside him. Soft gold hair cut very short remained deliciously attractive around a round face with china-blue eyes, a soft white, almost alabaster skin that made full red lips seem brilliant. She wore a pink tulle dress, very frothy with a square neckline that let two very round, very high twin mounds well over the edge. She could have been made of cotton candy and spun sugar, Fargo reflected.

Henson turned to her. "It's him, from this afternoon, Miss Thornbury," he said. "I was just about to throw him out."

"Were you?" the young woman said, her eyes taking in the big black-haired man, and Fargo smiled inwardly. Under that cotton-candy exterior was a quick, sharp mind. She had instantly caught the hollowness of Henson's bluster. Fargo watched the china-blue eyes move up and down his long frame with undisguised interest.

"Get my father and Dean," she said to Henson, not looking at him. "I'll be in the library."

Henson started away and she beckoned with her eyes to the big man before her. She went down a side corridor of the house and Fargo followed her into a room of book-lined shelves, deep leather chairs covered with tan hides. She turned to him inside the room, the china-blue eyes surveying him again.

"Skye Fargo . . . the Trailsman," she murmured, and watched the surprise touch his face. "Sheriff Tracy was here. He told us about you."

"Sheriff Tracy always report to you?" Fargo asked mildly.

She smiled, a quick, flashing smile that curled the bright-red lips. "Hardly. He stopped here just as he stopped at Amity Sawyer's, where he met you, to tell us he didn't want any more trouble," she said.

Fargo weighed the answer. It was reasonable enough, he concluded. He set aside the fact that reasonable things aren't always what they seem. For the moment.

She laughed, a soft little sound. "You're a suspicious man, Fargo. I like that," she said.

"Why?" he asked mildly.

"They're never fools, and I detest fools," she said, her

voice full of light amusement, but he caught the edge of strength in it. "I'm Janet Thornbury," she said. "I'm glad you stopped by. We were talking about trying to find you after Sheriff Tracy left."

"Who is we?" Fargo asked.

The door opened before she could answer and Fargo's eyes went to the two men. The older came in first, a straight tall man with an autocratic face accustomed to looking down at people, a sharp nose and hard eyes, yet a handsome man, his hair still dark. The younger man was slender, echoes in his face of the older man's imperiousness but with less strength, a hint of meanness in tight, narrow lips.

"My father, Richard Thornbury, and my brother, Dean," Janet introduced. "This is the Trailsman, the man Sheriff Tracy told us about," she added. Fargo saw the older man's face soften some into politeness.

"Well, this is a coincidence, I'd say," Richard Thornbury remarked, his voice authoritative.

"I presume you've come about the incident today," Dean Thornbury said with a smile.

"Don't know that I'd call trying to lynch a man an incident," Fargo said mildly, and saw the girl break into a smile, a tiny laugh following it.

"Bravo," she cut in. "Our use of words is so revealing, isn't it?"

Fargo gave her a quick glance of approval. She was beaming, pleased at the moment.

"I withdraw the word," Dean said. "Henson is often carried away with himself."

"When he saw Amity Sawyer running Joseph Todd off our land, he just took matters into his own hands," Richard Thornbury added.

"You saying you wouldn't have gone along with him on it?" Fargo asked, keeping his voice amenable.

"That's right. I might have stopped her, but nothing

26

more," Richard Thornbury said. "I've a philosophy that if a slave is so unhappy here that he wants to run away, I say let him go. He'll be nothing but trouble to keep."

It was another exercise in reasonableness, Fargo noted. Within the framework of their political beliefs, the Thornburys seemed to trade in reasonableness. Dean Thornbury's voice cut into his thoughts. "Surely you're not here to become involved in the complex issues being fought out in the territory," the man said.

"No, I'm not on any crusade, if that's what you mean," Fargo said.

"More or less." Dean Thornbury smiled.

"But I do want to see that old man left alive," Fargo said. "Just as a plain, ordinary human thing to do. I was drawn into it today and I want to see that come out of it."

"Well, he's gone from here. We've no interest in him any further," Dean Thornbury answered.

"Somebody has," Fargo said crisply. "He's been marked by the slave hunter." He let his eyes sweep the two men. The Thornbury patriarch let his lips purse out in apparent surprise and Dean Thornbury smiled.

"You think we gave in his name," he said.

"The thought crossed my mind," Fargo answered quietly.

"Logical enough, but entirely wrong. We did not give his name," Dean said.

"Somebody did," Fargo commented.

"Not necessarily," Dean Thornbury said, and Fargo felt his brows lift in surprise. "The slave hunter is very well informed. He often picks out his own targets. Usually they are those he feels are in some way a symbol to others. I can see why he would choose Joseph Todd, especially as Amity Sawyer is involved. She's something of a symbol around here, too. But we had nothing to do with it, I assure you."

27

Dean Thornbury sounded convincing. So did the elder Thornbury. Maybe they were telling the truth, Fargo reflected. He couldn't dismiss the possibility. But he couldn't swallow it whole, either—not yet, anyway. "You say you wanted to find me. Why?" he asked, glancing at Janet Thornbury.

"My idea"—she smiled brightly—"when I heard about you. Father agreed."

"We want to hire you to do a job for us. It'll be good pay, I assure you," Richard Thornbury said. "I've had to slow down, doctor's orders, and Dean and Janet have taken over company business. We market a variety of products, many made from our own raw materials and in our own mills—dry goods, hides, cotton dresses and shirts, fancy leather, imported silks brought up from New Orleans by riverboat. Dean travels all over finding new markets, new communities, and people to handle our things."

"Finding new outlets is no good unless we can deliver to them," Dean Thornbury took up. "We need someone to map out the best trails, the best passages and routes for our wagon shipments. We figure you can do that job for us."

"We need the routes with the least chance of Indian attacks, the best alternatives in case of trouble, those with enough waterholes along the way, those that can be used in winter," Richard Thornbury said. "Janet will be on the road a lot, too, and you'd report to her. It's her job to set up some kind of schedule for deliveries based on the information you bring her."

"I've three regions waiting now," Janet Thornbury said. "I'd like to start working with you immediately on them." Tiny pinpoints of light danced inside the china-blue eyes and Fargo let her know he caught their silent message with a hint of a smile.

"Five hundred dollars a month," he heard Richard

Thornbury say, and he made no effort to conceal surprise.

"That's a powerful lot of money," he admitted.

"New outlets and new markets aren't worth a tinker's damn if we can't get the goods there safely and regularly," the elder Thornbury boomed. "We need a man with your talents and we'll pay for it."

"We figure it'll take about two months of your time, to start with," Dean Thornbury said.

"We must be getting back to our guests," Richard Thornbury cut in. "Janet can answer any other questions. I hope you'll do the job for us." He paused for a moment. "I figure you as a man who knows a good opportunity when he sees one. You don't have to like a man's politics to like his money, I've always said."

He smiled, turned abruptly, and strode from the room. Dean Thornbury nodded pleasantly and followed his father out. Fargo turned to the figure in shimmering pink, saw the little smile on her red lips, a toying, slightly superior little smile.

"You're still a suspicious man and I still like that," she said.

"And all that spun-sugar outside is a mask you wear," Fargo said. "You're sharp as a tack underneath."

"We all wear masks. Taking them off can be fun," she said, and once again the china-blue eyes danced. "You did your good deed," she said, and he grunted silently in admiration. She could pick up the unsaid with intuitive acuteness.

"I still want to see that old man safe," he commented.

The little smile stayed, quietly tantalizing. "That's your business," she said. "But I think I can find you a more rewarding crusade."

Fargo allowed a half-smile. "I imagine maybe you could. I'll come by in the morning with my answer," he told her.

A shaft of light caught at the short blond hair and made it glisten as she inclined her head for an instant, and the little smile told him she had no doubt about his answer. "In the morning," she echoed as she left him in the foyer, and he watched her turn away, her movements quick yet graceful, the round, high breasts swinging in unison. He stepped outside into the night and Henson, on the portico, glowered at him as he left. He rode the pinto slowly down the road, letting thoughts take their own shapes.

The money was not the kind a man turned down and Janet Thornbury was not something to pass by. She added intriguing dimensions to the job, but the offer itself continued to pull at him. Was it just what it seemed on the surface? Or was it something more? Were they being clever, thinking to keep him busy and under their thumb? Riding the land to find trails and passages for Janet Thornbury was one way to keep a man from doing other things. Fargo let the thought hang in his mind. Was that really what they wanted out of the offer? Fargo's lips curled in a half-smile. Two could play at that game. Working with Janet and her brother might just be the best way to help Joseph Todd find safety. Maybe the Thornburys knew only what they had said they did about the slave hunter. But maybe they knew a lot more. The job could be one way to find out. Fargo grunted and let his thoughts go to Janet Thornbury. She seemed apart from the others, cut from a different cloth. She'd taken quick delight in spearing her brother at his use of words. There'd been almost a contemptuousness in her manner. And under the spun-sugar exterior there was a fiercely independent determination. And something more, made clear by her remarks to him and the hardly veiled promises of the china-blue eyes. Janet Thornbury made the offer worth its while all by herself, Fargo reflected.

By the time he reached the darkened Sawyer house straddling the end of the road, his mind was made up. It was too intriguing a parlay to turn down, three birds with one stone, a chance for good money, good pussy, and a good deed all rolled into one. He stabled the pinto, entered the house, and found the dim hallway, then the first room, pushed the door in, and found a modest room with a single bed, a dresser, and a kerosene lamp. He didn't turn the lamp on, undressing to his shorts in the pale shaft of moonlight that filtered through the lone window. He lay down across the bed, still thinking about his visit to the Thornbury place when he heard the doorknob being slowly turned. The big Colt .45 was in his hand instantly, his finger resting against the trigger.

His eyes, blue quartz, watched the door push open slowly as he rested on one elbow on the bed, the Colt trained on the doorway. He felt his finger relax as the figure appeared in the doorway, brown hair hanging loose, a thin cotton nightgown that left her shoulders bare, tied in the center of the neckline with a loose drawstring knot. She halted in the doorway, the pale moonlight giving her a wraithlike air.

Fargo slipped the Colt into the holster again where it hung from the bedpost, his eyes moving down the length of the cotton nightgown. It hung straight, yet clung to her legs at the sides, offering the outline of long thighs. She pulled the door closed softly, stepped to the edge of the bed, and her glance moved along the beauty of his hard-muscled body, finally lifting to meet his faintly curious gaze.

"Surprised?" she asked almost truculently.

"Some," he allowed.

"That makes two of us," Amity Sawyer said.

"Why, then?" he asked.

"What if I said it was you?" she asked.

"Say it," he answered.

A trace of bitterness crept into her tone. "You send out sparks. Your eyes don't just look at a woman, they reach inside her. They make her recognize how long she's been lonely and hungry and how much wanting there is all bottled up." She paused, searched his face. "You don't believe me, do you?" she said. "Or have you just heard all that too many times?"

"Maybe some of both. Anything else?" he asked blandly.

Her brow furrowed. "Meaning what?"

"I don't want you doing the right thing for the wrong reasons," he said.

"I didn't think reasons would bother you any," she returned with sarcasm in her voice.

"They don't. I just want you to know it's been tried before and it doesn't work with me," Fargo said calmly.

"What doesn't work?" She frowned.

"Pussy bargaining," he said.

He heard the sharp gasp from her, saw her hand flash out. He moved his face a fraction and the slap only grazed his cheek.

"Bastard," she hissed. "I didn't come here for that."

"Talk won't prove it," he said, pulled the drawstring bow with two fingers. The nightgown fell open like a curtain, drew back to reveal her breasts, long, as they had seemed under her clothes, turning full and round at the bottom, twin pears at the ends of long vines, a surprisingly graceful loveliness. He reached out both hands, cupped both mounds, felt their softness, and he heard the breath suck in from her, a long half-moan. He pushed the rest of the nightgown down and she sank down on the bed, drew her legs up in a gesture of modesty. He refused to permit it, spun her around, pushed long full thighs down, and her very black, very dense triangle lifted slightly.

"Oh, God," he heard her say, and he moved his torso over her legs as she tried to draw them up again. His face pressed into the two soft pear-shaped mounds and she gasped out again as her hands reached into his hair, pulling. He brought his lips up to her face, saw her mouth trying to protest, ended it with a harsh, demanding kiss, his tongue reaching quickly through her parted lips. Her moment of second thoughts vanished as her tongue answered, turning, darting, pushing back. He felt her hands moving down along his ribs, across his hips, and he half-turned for her, let her close around the sword of flesh that she wanted inside her. "Oh, oooooh . . . oh, God," she murmured, pressed her hand tight around him.

He let his hand find the dark and tangled warmth of her, press into the sweet and secret places, and she was wet with wanting. He drew his fingers slowly, caressing the very tip of the moist darkness, and she screamed, her hips lifting, flat abdomen rising into the air. "Oooooh, oh, yes, yes, please, oh, God please," she murmured, the words sliding into each other, becoming a sweet moaning call.

Her hands clawed at his buttocks, drawing him over her, and the long-limbed frame rose up again, legs wrapping around him. He rested against the very edge of her and she half-screamed in anticipation, pushed upward against him, and again her scream came at the soft-hard touch of him against her. Slowly he slid forward, smooth wet welcome waiting for him, and her breath came from her in a long, low gasp. He moved again, backward, almost to the very edge, almost out of her, and she half-screamed in protest. "No, no, oh, no," she cried out, and then, as he slid forward again, "aaaaaaaah . . . oh, yes . . . aaaah."

He gathered one long, pear-bottomed breast in his mouth and she gasped in pleasure, and her long body

33

half-twisted, first one way, then the other, moved with him, suddenly hurrying. He let her set the rhythm and the tiny cries came with his every smooth, sliding thrust to match her upward urges. He felt her moving toward a climax, slowed, and she screamed again in protest even as she worked furiously under him. But he slowed her, then began again to bring her up, and once again her gaspings were feverish as he moved with her and this time he let her cross that invisible line of feverish wanting, find that explosion waiting inside her. Hands clasped around his neck suddenly and her back lifted from the bed, her entire body frozen in space until the cry welled up from her, burst forth, and he hung in the air inside her as the cry became a gasping moan, the moan a wail, and the wail a half-sob.

"No, oh, no," she murmured as the explosion of ecstasy swept away as suddenly as it had come and she fell back onto the bed, still holding him inside her. He soothed her murmured protests by caressing the soft, full-bottomed breasts with his lips, and finally he lay beside her, his eyes taking in the long-limbed body, almost too angular, yet terribly attractive in its own ways. As with her face, the bits and parts all came together to make their own loveliness: square, strong shoulders, hips that held a certain lean sensuousness, a long, smooth rib cage, an almost concave abdomen, and beneath it, the thick, dense black bush that invited exploring.

He let his fingers move slowly through it and her long thighs fell open at once, straightening out, then pulling back, moving open wider, the eternal invitation issued without conscious thought, the body making its own answer. His hand moved slowly below the dense bush, felt her wet at once, waiting.

"Yes . . . uuuuaaaa . . . yes. . . ." The whispered sounds came from her, and he felt her hands pulling at him again, the wide hips twisting to welcome him. He took her again and this time she hardly stopped moaning in soft, almost soundless gasps until she exploded again when he let her. She clung to him until she fell back to finally lay still, her stomach heaving as she drew in deep drafts of air, the senses surfeited.

Finally she pushed herself up on one elbow, her hand on his chest. "Satisfied?" she asked.

"I think that's my question," he said.

A tiny smile pulled at her lips. "I mean, you think it was just bargaining," she answered.

"No," he conceded. "It was real, wanting and needing."

Her hand traced idly across his chest. "Stay, Fargo," she murmured. "Help me and help Joseph."

"My way, if I can, not the way you want it," he told her.

Her face took on the hint of a pout. "Whatever that means," she muttered.

"It means just what it said," he answered.

The half-pout stayed on her face. "You see the Thornburys?" she asked.

He nodded. "Didn't find out a lot."

"I told you that much," she sniffed.

"Richard Thornbury said they didn't care any more about what happens to Joseph," Fargo told her.

"Hell they don't," she snapped at once. "You don't believe that, do you?" She frowned.

"I'll make my mind up later," he said, and saw the disapproval touch his face.

"Was she there?" Amity muttered.

"Janet Thornbury?" Fargo asked, and Amity nodded, her face set. "Yes," he answered. "She's not like the others, I'm thinking. She's different."

"Bull," Amity snapped out. "They're all the same, all Thornburys, all with the same ideas. She just tries to make out she's above it all."

"I think she is. Underneath, I think she and her kin don't see eye to eye," he ventured. Amity's glare showed her complete rejection of his words. "They offered real good money, top dollar, to do a job for them," Fargo slid out. She half-rose on one elbow, waited, the hazel eyes darkening. "I took it," he said.

"You what?" she breathed.

"I took it," he repeated softly.

As though she were a spring uncoiling, she hurtled at him, nails clawing at his face. "Bastard. Rotten, stinking, son-of-a-bitch bastard," she screamed.

He ducked her nails, rolled to one side as, on her knees on the bed, she leaped at him again, a naked fury. Twisting away from her clawing hands, he caught her around the middle, tossed her to one side, and she landed on her rear, long legs flying upward, and he caught a moment's glimpse of the place that had welcomed him only minutes earlier.

"Stinking bastard," she hissed, coming down on her back, rolling, striking out, and he blocked the round-house swing. He grabbed her arm, turned it, and she cried out. "Owooo, goddamn you," she gasped, and he twisted again, turned her on her side. Wriggling like a fish, she kicked out at him and he had to let go of her to avoid a heel in his belly. She started to pull herself up again, her rear to him, and he planted one foot hard against it, pushed, and she went sprawling facedown across the bed.

He was after her at once, flinging her around on her back, and he felt her try to bring her knee up into his groin. "Rotten, rotten bastard," she gasped, and she was all raging fury. "I'll kill you," she hissed.

He took her by the hair, bounced her head up and down on the bed, and heard her gasping her breath. "Now that's enough out of you, dammit," he growled, finally stopping, and she glared up at him as she fought to draw in air. He bounced her again. "You hear me? Knock it off," he ordered angrily, holding her body down with his.

She found breath. "Get away from me," she hissed.

"When I'm ready," he returned, his hands holding her arms immobile against the bed. The long, pear-shaped breasts fell to the sides, improperly provocative. "Now you're going to listen to me," he growled.

"No," she said, tried to bring her head around to bite at his wrist, found it was impossible, and fell back onto the bed.

"I took the job to try and help you and Joseph," Fargo said.

"Working for those rotten, slave-owning Thornburys? Get out of my house," she flung back, tried to get her arms free. He tightened his grip. "Owoooo!" she cried. "Damn you."

"Will you listen to me, dammit?" he said.

She tried to twist her nakedness from him, finally gave up to draw in long breaths of air as she glared up at him.

"Where'd you ever get the name Amity?" he commented, keeping his grip on her.

"Not for the likes of you," she hissed. "And to think I came to you, let you touch me."

"I'll do it again, here and now, if you don't listen to me," he threatened.

He saw a touch of fright come into the hazel eyes. "You wouldn't," she said.

"Hell I wouldn't." He grinned down at her. "You might be even better with all that rage boiling inside you."

Her eyes peered at him, uncertainty in their depths. He moved his hips, let himself come hard against the dense bush under him.

"All right, I'll listen," she said.

He didn't shift position as he spoke to her. "Maybe I

37

can find out something about this slave hunter working for the Thornburys," he said. "Maybe something to help you and Joseph."

She made a derisive sound. "Hah! They'll use you and spit you out," she said.

"I doubt that," Fargo said calmly. "I figure it's worth a try. Your problem is you can't see straight for all the hate inside you."

"I can see that you're going to take their rotten blood money," she answered.

"So what, if taking it can help you," he countered.

He felt her arms relax, her body grow softer as the fury slid away from her, and he released his grip, pulled back, and let her sit up. She reached out, drew the nightgown to her, and covered herself with it.

"I can't see you that way now?" Fargo grinned.

"That's right," she snapped. "Go look at Janet Thornbury. She'll not give you the time of day."

"I'll take the time of night," he said.

She glowered from a corner of the bed, the nightgown held tightly in front of her. "I ask you for help and you turn me down, but you take the Thornburys' money. That's all any of this means to you," she said accusingly.

"The money's only part of it, I told you," he said.

"You expect me to believe that?" she glowered.

"Yes, dammit," he answered.

She continued to glower at him across the bed. "That's asking too much," she said.

"Work on it," he growled. "Meanwhile, I'm going to get some sleep." He lay back across the bed and she stayed motionless, a dim shape in the pale light coming through the window.

"Maybe you do want to help in your own way," he heard her murmur. "But it won't work, you wait and see."

"I'll do just that, wait and see," Fargo said, looked up

at the ceiling, and put his arms behind his head. He heard her move, felt the mattress give, and expected to hear her steps sliding across the floor. Instead, he felt her hair against his arm, then her head nestling into the hollow of his shoulder. Her skin touched his, no night-gown in the way, the long breasts resting against his ribs.

"Good night, Fargo," she whispered.

"Damn, you're a funny little thing," he said, frowning.

"And you're a strange, stubborn man," she answered, and pushed herself harder against him. He put his arm down, cradled her to him, and heard the little satisfied sigh from her.

3

Fargo, in the barn, had just finished saddling the pinto when she appeared in the doorway, a steaming cup of coffee in one hand. She held it out to him. She had changed into a gray shirt and a gray skirt. The hint of a glower in her eyes told him she understood the smile that touched his lips. The last time he saw her she was nakedly lovely in his arms.

She had come awake with the dawn just as he had and her long legs had moved at once to grasp him as she lifted herself, swung her hips over him. She had rubbed the dense, thick bush back and forth against him, and he had responded at once. "Oh, God, oh, yes," she'd murmured as she felt him rising to meet her. She had stayed atop him, sinking down onto him with a low, almost sobbing cry of sheer ecstasy. She had done the rest almost all by herself, pressing, writhing, twisting atop him, taking all of him, drawing up, then plunging herself down again to rest her warm wetness against his pelvic bones until the moment came and she buried the scream into his chest, clung there, and, minutes later, fell limply alongside him. She lay there, legs still half atop him, as the sun slowly crept across the windowsill.

"Nice way to start the day," he remarked as her breath became normal again.

"I don't expect another morning like this for a long

time. I figured to make the most of it," she said, and didn't hide the grim acceptance in her voice.

"You did," he said. She didn't answer and he rose and went to the washbasin. He heard her leave, moving quickly on bare feet, and she was gone when he turned around. He'd finished washing, dressed, and gone to the stable, and it was all in his eyes now as he looked at her.

"I'm not sorry for anything," Amity said, lifting her chin. "Haven't changed my mind about what you're going to do, either."

"Didn't expect you would," he said, sipped the coffee, and enjoyed the bracing tang of it. "What's your next move?" he asked.

She hesitated a moment, decided to go on. "I'll meet with Frank Hasslet and Bill Conway. They're in charge of this part of the underground railroad, though everybody helps as much as they can. We take the runaways halfway to the Missouri border, then others take them the rest of the way. Once in Missouri there's another group that takes over and that's how it goes till they reach Illinois." She paused. "It takes planning. Everything must be all set up all along the way."

"For those who make it," Fargo said.

Her eyes were touched by pain. "For those who make it," she echoed. "I'll have to tell Frank and Bill about the mark of the slave hunter. They'll tell me when they can fit Joseph in. There are others scheduled ahead of him."

"I'll stop back tonight. You can tell me the rest then," Fargo said, and again he saw the instant of hesitation touch her eyes. "I can't help if you don't level with me," he said.

She nodded, her lips tightening. "I guess not. I guess there's a time for trusting," she said. He handed her the empty cup and swung onto the pinto, watched her slip from the barn, the long brown hair swinging behind her.

41

When he rode from the barn, she was inside the house and he saw Joseph and Jimmy waiting.

"Will you be coming back, Mr. Fargo?" Jimmy asked.

"I expect so," Fargo said, his eyes moving to the gray-haired black man. "Be careful, Joseph," he said, and Joseph Todd's face was made of understanding. Fargo rode on, turned at the two pin oaks, and made for the Thornbury place. The big house looked even more like a transplanted Georgia mansion in the daylight. Black gardeners and handymen were busy tending to their chores as he halted the pinto in front of the hitching post.

Janet Thornbury appeared from around the corner, short blond hair sparkling in the morning sun. Under a white shirt buttoned to the neck, her bustline was still very high and very round. Her father followed her into sight, riding crop in hand, a stableboy leading a gray, long-legged hunter behind him.

"So you've come, Fargo. What's the word?" the man said in his authoritative manner.

"I figure it'll be easy money for me," Fargo said.

"Excellent," the man boomed as the stableboy helped him get a leg up into the stirrups. In the saddle, he looked down at Fargo, his smile one of confident imperiousness. "I knew you weren't the kind of man to turn down good money," he said. "Janet will go over the details with you." He sent the horse forward and five riders met him at the gate, Henson one of them, as he led the way out across the flatland.

Fargo turned to Janet, aware that her china-blue eyes were watching him with undisguised amusement. "Father can be so happily wrong, can't he?" she remarked.

"Maybe," he said cautiously.

She laughed, the velvety sound softly appealing. "Come into the library," she said, and he followed her into the house. She brought out a manila folder, rifled

42

through various pieces of paper in it, and halted at one. "This is the first one, the area around Miller Creek. Dean is going back to see his contacts there," she said.

"That's in the Owl River Basin," Fargo commented. "Hell, Owl Bend is the only town there. That's wild country."

"Some people are trying to set root. They're the ones we want to carry our products with them," Janet said. "I'll be in Owl Bend in a few days. I'll expect you."

"I could be a week at least," Fargo said.

"Make a preliminary survey," she said, and her eyes suddenly wore invisible veils. "We can go over it together."

"Whatever you say," he agreed, saw the tiny smile touch her lips.

She walked outside with him and he saw a bay mare saddled and waiting for her. "I'll ride a ways with you," she said.

"I'm going into Hillsville. I want two new shoes put on the pinto," Fargo said. He had just swung into the saddle when Dean Thornbury appeared. Out of the fancy dress clothes he seemed harder, his tight mouth crueler.

"I hear you're taking the job for us," he said, smiled at the question in Fargo's eyes. "Stableboys talk," he said. "I'm sure you'll give us all we need."

"I hope so," Fargo heard Janet say and cast a quick glance at her. The round, soft face was expressionless, but the china-blue eyes danced. She swung in beside him as he rode away.

"You enjoy playing games," he remarked.

"Some," she said.

"Some can be right dangerous," he said.

"I like only that kind," she said.

He glanced at her smooth-cheeked, pretty face, the short nose, the alabaster skin that added to the spun-

43

sugar exterior. The high busts pressed the white shirt into two smooth mounds, not even the tiniest dot spearing the taut material. "I'd think a gal like you would have had every man at that party panting after her," Fargo slid out.

"They're panting," she said almost grimly.

"But you're not," he finished.

"Give the man a cigar," she said sharply. "They're not men, they're spineless excuses for men. They're all full of good manners, stupid ideas and their hollow associations. I'm tired of men who are afraid of me."

"They scared of you as a Thornbury or as a woman?" he asked.

"I don't know and I don't care," she snapped, reined up as they reached a fork in the road. "I'm heading upland," she said, her eyes sharp on him. "Owl Bend, in a few days," she said.

"What if I don't make it?" he asked, letting a smile go with the question.

"I'll think you're afraid of me, too," she said.

"You know better," he said, and watched her wheel the horse and ride away, not a tall girl, the stirrups shortened for her legs. But she was a seething little whirlwind inside, he mused. Janet Thornbury was very much her own woman and very different from her father and brother. Amity Sawyer was wrong about her, he reflected. And if Janet Thornbury was playing the tease, she'd learn about that mistake. He prodded the pinto on toward Hillsville, broke into a canter as the town came into sight.

While the smithy fashioned two new shoes for the pinto, Fargo went to the general store, stocked his saddlebag with hardtack and pemmican, and added a bag of grits. He asked directions to the sheriff's office and was told it was at the far end of town. As he strolled in that direction, he heard the sound of rifle fire, evenly spaced, deliberate shooting. Target practice, he grunted. He reached the sheriff's office, peered through the window. It was empty inside and a shot echoed from behind the building. He strolled around to the back to see Sam Tracy, Ned standing by, taking rifle practice. A row of thin reeds were hung from a distant tree and Fargo watched the man blow each thin reed away without a miss in a display of expert marksmanship. The sheriff was using a new Winchester .44 rifle with one of the new front barrel sights for long-range accuracy.

"Damn good shooting," Fargo said appreciatively, and Sam Tracy turned, lowered the rifle.

"Thanks. I try to stay sharp," he said, and Fargo heard the pride quick to come into his voice. "Only one man I know who can outshoot me and that's Dean Thornbury. We have a two-man shoot at least twice a year." Sam Tracy's gray eyes took on a glint. "Want to give it a try?" he asked the big black-haired man. "I'd like to see you shoot."

"Maybe some other time," Fargo said pleasantly.

The sheriff nodded. "Hear you sort of switched sides," he remarked.

"I wouldn't put it that way," Fargo answered evenly. "Thornbury offered me good money to do a job for him, that's all. News travels fast around here."

"I try to keep on top of things," the man said with a hint of smugness.

"Not on top of the slave hunter, it seems," Fargo commented blandly, saw the sheriff's gray eyes narrow slightly.

Sam Tracy's smile was thin. "Not yet," he said. "It's a question of not having the manpower to do everything."

Fargo allowed him an understanding smile while he wondered whether it was a question of not trying too hard. Perhaps Sam Tracy was being paid a little extra to hold back. "Any ideas about this slave hunter?" Fargo asked. "You know all the members of the slave-owners' association."

"No ideas," the man said.

"It's sure as hell not one of the free-staters," Fargo said.

"Maybe no, and then again maybe yes," the sheriff said. Fargo threw him a sharp glance. "Ever hear of Judas?" Sam Tracy said.

Fargo continued to peer at him. It was an angle he'd not considered and he set the statement away for further thought. "Interesting," he murmured.

"Tell you another thing," Sam Tracy said. "It's somebody who takes it all very personal. I wouldn't like tangling with that kind of man if I were you."

"I'll remember the advice." Fargo smiled as he sauntered away. Sam Tracy was nobody's fool, he decided again, even as he wondered whose tightrope the man walked. Perhaps only his own, Fargo reflected, and then perhaps not. Sam Tracy would stay a question mark.

The smithy was finished when Fargo returned to the shop and he examined the pinto's feet, then paid the man and rode from Hillsville to where he could see the beginnings of the Owl River Basin. He didn't think he'd find a good trail anywhere through the basin; he grunted, turned the pinto, and headed back for Amity Sawyer's place. The afternoon was lowering when he reached the house, and Amity, at the door, watched him dismount. Her face was unsmiling, almost truculent, he saw.

"You all settled in working for the Thornburys?" she said, disdain in her voice.

"That's right, but I didn't come back here to talk about that," he said curtly. "What's with Joseph now?"

"There are two in line ahead of him. We're taking one tomorrow, Clarabelle Moore," Amity said.

"We?" Fargo questioned.

"I'll be along," she answered. "Clarabelle's only eighteen. She escaped from the Ranklin place after a wild chase. We've been hiding her ever since." Amity's lips tightened. "She's been marked by the slave hunter," she finished.

"How do you figure to take her?" Fargo asked.

"The plan is to go through the Owl River Basin. It's a route we've never used."

Fargo felt the furrow crease his brow. The Owl River Basin, he echoed silently. Dean Thornbury would be riding the area somewhere. Coincidences did happen. He'd seen that often enough. Yet this was too neat, too convenient. He let thoughts turn in his mind. Coincidence or connection? He couldn't dismiss either. He focused back on Amity. "How are you moving the girl?" he asked.

"Frank Hasslet's baggage wagon. Three inside it besides Clarabelle and four outriders," Amity said.

"Why so many?"

"The slave hunter doesn't always work alone," Amity answered.

Fargo frowned, surprise sweeping over him first, then another thought. "That might be of help," he murmured.

"Why?" Amity asked.

"Somebody meets with him. Somebody must know who he is. Maybe a handful of people. I only need to get one to talk," Fargo said. "When do you leave?"

"Day after tomorrow, late afternoon," she said.

"I'll find you," he said. "I'm riding out now." He saw the flicker of disappointment touch her face. "Patience is a virtue, they tell me." He grinned.

"What would you know about virtue?" she flung back, spun on her heel, and disappeared inside the house.

Fargo mounted the pinto and rode away at a fast canter. Amity Sawyer was a crusader with a bent lance, fighting a rear-guard action at best. It would've been

47

easy to stay, but he hadn't the time to waste. He had a lot of ground to cover if he was going to have answers for Janet Thornbury ready and have the time to find Amity and her friends. He wanted to be there if the slave hunter struck. Maybe he'd get lucky and wrap this business up fast. He could devote all his attention to Janet Thornbury then. He smiled.

The night came and he kept riding, halted only when he reached the edge of the Owl River Basin where the land began its slow dip. He made camp, slept soundly under the night sky, and woke with the new day. He found a trickle of a stream in which to wash and breakfasted on a large cluster of raspberries. When he sat astride the pinto again, his eyes swept the land before him. The Owl River Basin was a huge soup plate, dipping down with each edge rimmed in a circle too wide to take in with the naked eye. Within the huge soup plate of land there were a series of ridges and rises, dense foliage, mostly bur oak with their heavily lined bark. The town of Owl Bend sat off to his right, barely visible, near one edge of the basin like a fly sitting on the lip of a dish. He scanned the other line of the circular rim nearest him, the west edge. Amity and her runaway would be coming from that direction where a trail ran along the bottom of the basin just under the edge of the upward-sloping rim.

He moved the pinto forward, headed for the center of the Owl River Basin as his eyes scanned every side path and trail. He let the horse meander, made little notes in a small pocket-size notepad. By midday, he had made a fair-sized circle around the center part of the basin of land and his lips were held tight in displeasure. There wasn't a good trail anywhere in the Owl River Basin, except along the outer rims. The interior of the land was made of twists and snags and unexpected serrations of rock and ridges. Moreover, it was a perfect place for Indian ambush and it sat full in the middle of country through which the Pawnee, Osage, and sometimes the Kiowas held a long-running feud for territorial rights. There were settlers who tried to dig in here, he knew, but he considered them as either very brave or very stupid.

By nightfall, beside a small fire, he completed his notes on the few passageways he'd charted leading from the direction of Owl Bend to the far western rim of the basin, a tenuous line through ridge-studded land to the Chuck Hole section and one more path that circled the center of the basin to come in from the north side. So far as he was concerned, they were all rotten, and he was deciding that Dean Thornbury had a damn poor eye for new territories for his goods.

Fargo finally slept and by dawn was moving across to the far side of the basin of land. He squinted at the way the morning wind swooped down over him and it was just a little past midday when he halted by a brook, let the pinto drink and cool his ankles. Fargo closed his little notepad. Unless the Thornburys wanted to spend the time and the money to hack out a road, there wasn't one passage good for wagons in the Owl River Basin, he said to himself. And even if they did, it wouldn't be worth a damn except for the three months of good summer weather. In winter, the fierce snowstorms would fill the soup plate to the brim and only trappers and Indians would venture out. In the spring, the thaws would turn it into a small sea of mud and water. Janet Thornbury would get a damn poor report from him on the Owl River Basin. He sniffed, turned the pinto, and headed for the west rim.

By late afternoon, as he came into sight of the west rim of the basin, the shadows were lengthening. Not only the shadows, he noted, but a tower of thick white clouds with purple-gray bottoms, heavy thunderstorm clouds, and he watched their movement as he rode. Another hour or two and they'd be sweeping down over the west rim of the basin, he estimated. He increased speed, crested one of the many ridges, and hurried down the other side. A warning flash of lightning came from deep inside the towering mass of clouds, like the blink of a giant, baleful eye. He reached back with one hand, pulled the slicker from his saddlebag without slowing the pinto, and wriggled it over his shoulders. The lightning flashed again. It promised to be a severe one, he noted unhappily.

He was nearing the west rim as he halted atop a flat rock to scan the land and the road in the distance. Ridges and wiry underbrush made a series of steps and the ground had turned a mixture of red clay, he saw. The red-clay soil ran to the road and on the other side, turned dark brown again, he observed. He stayed on a small rise and began to move north until he espied the wagon on the road below, a half-mile or so ahead, and he sent the pinto into a gallop. He was almost abreast of it but atop the rise of land as the night and the storm began to roll over the land.

He shook his head in disgust. Two riders rode in front of the wagon and two behind and the wagon careened along the road, the two horses galloping at top speed. Stupid, he muttered silently. They should have been riding nice and easy, a baggage wagon and four outriders on its way someplace. If the slave hunter waited and watched someplace, he might pass up such a wagon, but he'd sure as hell zero in on a wagon racing wildly at top speed. Christ, they might just as well have put up a sign, Fargo thought, grimacing.

He could see Amity inside the wagon, long brown hair tossing, a rifle across her lap. A slender figure wrapped in a shawl sat beside her, a man positioned inside at the rear.

The rain began to fling itself at him as the last of the light faded and Fargo continued to ride parallel to the racing wagon below as his eyes swept the high ground of the rim. There was but a thin edge of light left when he glimpsed the three horsemen on the rim just ahead, rifles in hand, spread out a dozen yards apart. He saw them raise their rifles as he swore silently, sent the pinto racing down from the ridge and hurtling toward the road below. A tremendous thunderclap blotted out the sound of the rifle shots, but Fargo saw one of the outriders half-fall from the saddle and the others duck, bring up their own guns.

The darkness was on the land now and two thunder-claps were separated by bursts of lightning. The outriders were wheeling, firing upward wildly, Fargo saw, watched two of them whirl to train their guns on him as he raced in from the side. He lifted one hand up, waved furiously, and the men held back fire. "They're up on the rim," Fargo shouted as he reined up. "Move out some. You can't even see them from here," he said.

The men spurred their horses and moved out, and an-other burst of lightning gave them a brief chance to re-turn fire. The sharp sound of the rifle fire became a counterpoint to the tremendous thunderclaps as the outriders raced back and forth, firing blindly upward. But the riflemen on the ridge were firing with equal blindness. Fargo frowned.

He rode after the racing wagon as the rain came down in driving sheets. Inside the wagon, Amity was on one knee, trying to steady herself but unable to get off any kind of a shot in the jouncing wagon. Each flash of lightning flooded the scene with a split second of bril-liant light.

The riflemen atop the rim were still pouring down fire wildly, aimlessly, the outriders replying as best they could, and Fargo frowned as he rode beside the wagon

51

in the pelting rain. The attack didn't make any damn sense, he muttered to himself. He was still frowning into the storm-swept darkness when he reined up, the sinking feeling seizing him in the pit of the stomach. "Dammit, of course not," he spit out into the rain. The attack wasn't made to make sense. It was a diversion.

He wheeled the pinto, peered into the night, wiped rain from his eyes just as a flash of lightning cracked, bathed the moment in electric-blue light. Fargo heard the crack of the rifle just before the thunderclap's boom, saw the figure next to Amity pitch forward, the shawl ripping away. The moment plunged back into darkness as Fargo heard himself cursing. The shot hadn't come from the rim but from the other side, from one of the ridges. Another flash of lightning cracked the darkness into blue day and his eyes, sweeping the ridges, saw the rider, black mask, black clothes, black horse. The man was just wheeling the horse around, the rifle still in hand. Fargo saw the horse start to bolt away as the blackness returned to blot out all else.

"Goddamn," he swore into the wind, saw the wagon come to a halt. The distant ridge was too distant, the rider gone already, and the downpour washing away tracks. But Fargo turned the pinto, started to race up the sloping land toward the west rim where the three riflemen let go with a final volley. He thanked another lightning flash as it let him see the three riders splitting up, one racing back south, the other two starting north along the edge of the rim. Blackness wiped away the moment, but Fargo had seen enough, turned the pinto to climb at an angle so that when he reached the top of the rim he could hear the sucking clop of hooves fleeing the water-soaked ground.

The lightning was growing less frequent, but another flash let him glimpse the two riders in the distance, still galloping along the edge of the rim. They'd veer off soon onto the flatland, he anticipated, and he wheeled the pinto, cutting away from the rim of the basin to hurtle along the flatland. The move earned him fifty yards as the two horsemen finally left the edge of the basin to cut west. The rain had stopped as suddenly as it had come, and the moon appeared, looking out of place in its suddenness.

The horsemen were not far ahead and he saw one turn, suddenly aware of their pursuer. The other turned and Fargo saw both raise their rifles, fire almost as one. He let out a half-scream followed by a guttural gasp, fell forward against the saddle horn to lie flat over the pinto's withers, too flat to be a target.

"We got him," he heard the one man shout. They slowed their horses as the pinto neared. Fargo stayed limp and flat across the pinto's withers, his face against the wet fur of the horse's neck. The pinto kept running, almost directly at one of the riflemen. Fargo's figure draped lifelessly forward as the man brought his horse around, reached a hand out to seize the pinto's bridle. Fargo, leg muscles tensed, waited a moment longer, then hurtled from the saddle, a sideways, diving leap. It caught the rifleman completely by surprise, took him flying from the saddle. He hit the ground with Fargo atop him, the breath rushing out of him in a deep gasp.

He'd be a few moments recovering, Fargo knew, rolled from the limp figure, came up on his back with the big Colt .45 in his hand. He saw the second rider galloping at him, the rifle at his shoulder, drawing a bead on the figure on the ground. He never got the shot off as Fargo's Colt barked and a gaping hole tore open in the man's throat, on both sides as the bullet passed through his neck. Twin streams of red spurted from him and his mouth fell open. His hands clawed at his neck for a brief moment and then he toppled forward from the horse, lifeless before he hit the ground.

Fargo whirled, got to his feet as he saw the first man start to pull himself up, his breath returning. Fargo swung a looping right. It caught the man alongside the jaw, sent him falling backward again. Fargo was at him instantly as the man tried to reach for his six-gun. Fargo's foot kicked the gun out of his hand as he had it half drawn from the holster and the weapon slid across the wet ground. The man rolled, came onto his feet, head lowered, charged the big black-haired man who had come out of the storm-swept night.

Fargo's short uppercut cracked against his chin, sent him staggering backward, as much surprise as pain in his eyes. The man had a beefy face and Fargo smashed the nose into shapelessness with a crashing overhand right. The man fell backward, tried to roll aside, but Fargo seized him in one big hand, smashed him to the ground with another sledgehammer blow.

"Uuuh, oh, Christ," the man muttered as he lay prone, his face streaming blood.

"Talk to me," Fargo growled, and watched the man raise himself to a sitting position, rub his shirtsleeve across his bloodied and battered face.

"About what?" the man mumbled.

"The slave hunter," Fargo said.

"I don't know anything," the man muttered into his arm.

Fargo's backhand blow crashed into the side of his face and the figure half-twisted as it toppled backward.

"Ow, Jesus, no more," the man gasped into the dirt. Fargo's hand yanked him half up and around and he raised his fist to bring it down again. "I ain't lyin'," the man almost screamed.

"How'd you like a face nobody can put back together again?" Fargo asked.

"I'm telling you, I don't know anything," the man answered, pain and fear etched into his face. No act, Fargo decided, the fear too stark in the man's eyes.

"He hired you. You've got to know something," Fargo insisted, released his hold on the man, who promptly fell back onto one elbow, wiped the fresh blood from the side of his face with his other hand.

"No," the man spit out through swollen lips. "He hired us, but nobody ever saw him."

"How come?" Fargo pressed.

"I got a message, a note, the same as the others. It told us where to go and what to do and where we could pick up our pay," the man said. "It was the same on the other jobs we did. Nobody ever met him, talked to him."

"Where are you supposed to pick up your pay?" Fargo questioned.

"A drop about a quarter-mile from here. Everybody gets a different place," the man said.

"Get on your horse. You're going to pick it up and I'll be right behind you," Fargo said. "Maybe there'll be another note."

The man rose, pain in his face at the effort, and climbed slowly onto his horse. Fargo followed him on the pinto as the man led the way to a small cluster of black oak. The man pointed into the trees.

"Go on," Fargo said as he dropped back, drew the big Sharps rifle from its saddle case. He hung back more as he watched the man slowly ride to the edge of the oaks, start to swing himself down from the saddle. The moon threw a fair light now and Fargo's eyes swept the surrounding terrain, watching for any movement, the glint of gunmetal, a shadow among shadows. He returned his eyes to the man, who had gone to a log, reached his hand inside, and now drew out a roll of bills. Fargo's eyes swept the terrain again and then, satisfied it held no unpleasant surprises, he prodded the pinto forward.

He halted beside the log, swung from the saddle as the man counted his pay. "Nothing else?" Fargo asked.

"Nothing else," the man echoed, looked up with a surprised frown as the big black-haired man's hand closed over the money, drew it from his grip. "What're you doin'?" he rasped.

"There's a dead girl back there and you had a hand in it. This'll pay for burial expenses and whatever," Fargo said. He pushed the money into his pocket, turned back to the pinto, and ignored the man's roar of fury and protest.

"Son of a bitch," he heard the man curse, then another sound caught his ear, the flap of a saddlebag being flung open. He turned just in time to see the man pull a bowie knife from inside the saddlebag, charge after him with the blade upraised. Fargo ducked away from the first slashing swipe, avoided a second upward sweep.

"Bastard, I'll stick you through," the man snarled, and sent the bowie in a sideways sweep that made Fargo suck in his stomach to avoid the blade. The man was quick, following instantly with another slashing blow, and Fargo backpedaled, yanked the Colt from its holster.

"Drop the knife," he ordered. The bloodied face glared at him, the bowie upraised. "Don't be a fool, drop it," Fargo said.

The man hesitated a second longer and Fargo saw his arm begin to lower. The man brought his arm down, almost at his side, and Fargo pulled his finger from the trigger of the six-gun.

The man's move was lightning fast, a quick flick of his wrist, following through with his forearm, and the knife hurtled through the air in an underhand throw. Fargo had time only to twist away and he felt the bowie hit the edge of his shoulder, slicing open a tear in his shirt. He heard the man's roar, half-turned back to see the figure leaping at him, striking him off balance before he could bring the Colt around, and he felt himself go sprawling. The man's kick was off target, yet caught the side of his ribs, and Fargo rolled, kept rolling, avoided a second kick, and saw the figure diving at him, arms outstretched. The man landed atop him, one hand grabbing at the Colt, and Fargo brought a short blow up into the man's midsection, heard his grunt as he fell to the side.

Fargo reached one knee as the man dived for the knife on the ground, saw the man's hand close around the handle. Fargo fired, two quick shots, and saw the figure seem to stretch out, the man's shoulders lifting into the air for a moment, then dropping forward. Slowly his hand opened and the knife fell from his fingers. He shuddered again and lay still. Fargo rose, his mouth a tight line. "Stupid," he muttered at the inert figure, holstered the Colt, returned to the pinto, climbed into the saddle, and rode off at a fast trot.

He rode back along the rim, finally spied the wagon below, turned around, also headed back, no hurrying now, the horses walking slowly, the outriders alongside. Fargo headed the pinto down the sloping land to the road, and the outriders raised rifles, then lowered them as they recognized the Ovaro. He came to a halt beside the wagon, met Amity's mournful eyes. The slender figure inside the wagon lay covered completely with a blanket.

"The slave hunter is going to need two new guns," he said evenly.

"But he got away, of course," Amity said bitterly.

"There was no chance to get him. I hoped the others might tell me something," Fargo answered.

"Did they?" she asked skeptically.

"Nothing that'd help. He's very careful and very smart," Fargo admitted. He handed the money to her.

57

"Use it for whatever you want, burial, her relatives, your cause," he told her.

She didn't ask questions and stuffed the bills into a pocket in her skirt. "This will hurt. A lot of the younger ones were waiting to see if Clarabelle would make it," she said, dejection cloaking her voice.

"What next?" he asked.

"I'll be going home, till we try another run," she said.

"I'll be in touch, somehow," he said. She didn't answer and the driver flicked the reins, moved the horses forward. He watched the sad procession move off for a moment, turned the pinto, and headed across the west quadrant of the Owl River Basin toward the town of Owl Bend. His lips were a tight line as he rode and he let the wild and terrible night replay itself in his mind. The slave hunter had struck again, won again. He had struck and vanished, but not entirely without an imprint, Fargo pondered. There were pieces to sift, a few items to put together, not very much, yet a starting place.

He let the pinto move slowly over the still rain-soaked ground and began the process of sifting, weighing, evaluating. Fact and conjecture would overlap, run together, he knew, and he'd have to guard against mistaking one for the other. He sat back in the saddle and the lake-blue eyes narrowed in thought.

Piece number one was fact. It was first and foremost for the moment, above all else. The single shot that had ended Clarabelle Moore's flight, her hopes for freedom, and her life had been no ordinary shot. It had been the shot of an extraordinary marksman. Damn few people could shoot like that and Fargo's thoughts instantly went to the image of a tall, gray-eyed man blowing away thin little reeds in an incredible display of marksmanship. Sam Tracy could do that kind of shooting. And Sam Tracy had said that Dean Thornbury could outshoot him.

Fargo frowned, turned the statement over in his mind. Was it the truth, or a piece of fancy footwork, a false lead casually tossed out? He mulled the possibilities, set them aside for further thought.

Piece number two was next. Dean Thornbury was in the Owl River Basin. There'd been no secret made about that. He was in the area, and if he were, indeed, a crack shot, the two facts pointed only one way. Was Dean Thornbury the slave hunter?

The furrow on Fargo's brow dug deeper. The two facts pointed almost too hard. If Dean Thornbury was the slave hunter, would he have been so open, so bold in placing himself in the area? The slave hunter was proving to be a clever, painstaking, and very careful killer. He covered every track, cloaked every move. The hired guns had been testament to that. Would such a man openly place himself in the area? Or was its very openness another kind of cleverness, a double mask, a reverse play to make the obvious seem too obvious?

Only one fact was clear. He was quickly developing a bitter respect for the killer known as the slave hunter. And a deepening anger. "Damn," he swore softly. All because he'd tried to eat a sandwich under a tree. He swore again and rode the pinto into Owl Bend, most of the town darkened and asleep. A lone light bulb burned outside the front door of the lone hotel and he rode the pinto into the stable attached to the frame building. A sleepy-eyed stableboy appeared and blinked his eyes awake as he stared at the beauty of the Ovaro.

"Got a good stall for him?" Fargo asked.

"For him?" the stableboy echoed. "Anytime."

"Oats and water. Feed him light now, proper in the morning," Fargo ordered.

"Yes, sir," the boy said, leading the pinto away, his eyes still admiring the horse.

Fargo walked to the adjoining structure, passed under

the lone light bulb and into a dim foyer. An elderly man looked up from an equally elderly desk.

"Single," Fargo said.

"Sign here," the man said, pushing a registration card at him. "House rules. Everybody signs in," he explained almost apologetically.

"You have a Thornbury registered?" Fargo asked as he signed the card. The man shuffled through a handful of the small cards.

"Dean Thornbury?" he asked.

Fargo frowned in surprise. "Is he here?"

"Yep, come in about an hour ago," the man said.

The frown stayed on the Trailsman's brow. "You have a Janet Thornbury?" he asked.

The man rifled through the rest of the cards. "Yep, checked in this afternoon. Room nine," he said. "Two folks with the same name. Don't get that often." He handed Fargo a key on a wooden ring. "You've room three, second floor up," he said.

Fargo took his saddlebag to the room, lay down on the bed with the lamp out, his eyes narrowed in thought. He let ten minutes go by, rose, and made his way down and back to the stables. The stableboy, half-asleep against a bale of hay, came awake as he entered.

"Mr. Thornbury asked me to have a look at his horse," Fargo said.

"I rubbed him down good, the way he wanted," the boy said quickly. "That horse was real lathered up. He'd done some hard riding."

Fargo smiled. "I'm sure you did. He asked me to check out his fetlock. Seems he's got a half-limp."

"Second row, stall three," the boy said with a glance of relief.

Fargo moved away, down the second row of stalls, halted at the third one. A dim light from a kerosene lamp hanging from a ceiling beam gave him just enough light.

His eyes moved over the horse. No black stallion, he grunted, a red roan. That didn't mean all that much. He could have easily switched horses. It was likely, from what he had learned of the slave hunter's careful planning.

Fargo reached down, lifted the horse's left foreleg, scraped pieces of soil wedged into the cleft of the frog, got a little more from the wedge under the calkin, enough to tell him what he wanted to know. He stepped closer to the high lamp, crumbled the caked bits of soil between his fingers. Red clay, he murmured silently, stared at the pieces of soil, let them slowly fall from his hand as he walked from the stable.

Dean Thornbury had not only been in the Owl River Basin, Fargo pondered. He had been at the scene itself, ridden the red-clay land that bordered the one side of the road. No proof of anything more, Fargo realized. Dean Thornbury could have ridden the area earlier, or later. The stableboy had said the red roan had been ridden hard. Why? To get away from the area after horses had been switched? Or just to get away from the thunderstorm? Once again, possibilities more than proof. But the pieces were becoming more interesting. If he could put enough together, he might have a whole picture.

Fargo halted, his hand on the doorknob. The answers he needed wouldn't be his this night, but maybe he could get the answer to one question. He turned, started down the hallway.

4

Peeling gold paint barely marked the number 9 on the door and he knocked softly. In moments he heard the sound of movement inside the room, the faint glow of a lamp being turned up reaching out from under the door. "Who is it?" her voice said, velvety more than sleepy.

"Fargo," he said quietly.

The door opened and she peered out at him, a tiny frown touching her face as she surveyed him. The short blond hair caught glints from the lamplight and she wore a frilly blue nightdress with a lace collar. The spun-sugar exterior was still very much there as she stood before him, and so was the cool determination behind the china-blue eyes.

"Asleep?" he asked blandly.

"No," she said, the china-blue eyes still studying him. "I expected you earlier. I was wondering if you were going to arrive."

"Wondering or worrying?" he asked, stepping into the room.

Her eyes narrowed a fraction. "Wondering," she said.

"Liar," he answered. She didn't reply, let the door close. He espied a thin string at the frilly lace of the nightdress, pulled it, and the lace collar came open, down to the swell of her breasts. He smiled, watched her hand raise to cover the opening, let his eyes go to her mouth, the red lips slightly parted.

"No," she murmured. "You take a lot for granted."

"You play games," he said.

"You said maybe it was only that," she reminded.

"I know better now," he told her.

"What makes you so sure?" she returned, frowning.

"Ask me later," he said, pushed her hand away from the lace collar, watched the nightdress come open further. He pulled it open the rest of the way and her breasts came free of the garment. Not all that large, they were beautifully round and high, deliciously provocative mounds, very flat nipples, very pink with equally pink tiny circles around each. She made a fluttery attempt to pull the nightdress closed, but his hand stopped her, closed around one breast, rubbed across the flat little tip.

"Oh," she gasped. "Oh, God." She wriggled her hips and the rest of the nightdress fell to the floor. She stood as if transfixed as he shed clothes, his eyes moving across her young, fresh nakedness, rounded hips, a full little belly that thrust forward boldly and, below it, a light-colored, sandy triangle, modest, edges flattening against the inside of thighs that might someday tend to fat but now were only sensually full. She moved back, toward the bed, as he dropped the last of his clothes and her glance fastened on the throbbing power already thrusting out toward her. "Oh, Jesus," she murmured, suddenly fell forward toward him, seizing him, pulling him toward her.

He fell over the edge of the bed with her and her legs were around him at once, the little rounded belly lifting upward. Her hands clasped around his neck, pulled his head forward to her breasts. She let out a little screaming sound as he pulled on first one, then the other. He wasn't inside her, but she was lifting and pumping, pushing up for him, and he felt the wetness of her against him.

"Oh, Christ, take me, take me, Jesus, now, now," she

63

gasped out, and there was a franticness in her wanting, almost a panic.

He felt her mouth against his chest, biting, and he pushed her back. Her round face came against him again, her hands suddenly caressing, and she moaned as her legs moved up and down the back of his thighs. "Please," she managed to say as if it were a word that came hard to her. It probably did, he thought abstractly as he let his hand find the dark wetness of her and she thrust upward against him at once, a continuous series of violent thrustings, and she was making little throaty sounds.

He pushed hard and she cried out, but there was pleasure in the pain and he halted, held back a moment, then rammed hard into her. She seemed to explode with wild pumping and he drew back, rammed hard again, again and again.

"Yes, oh, yes, yes, yes, yes, Jesus . . . Jesus, yes, yes," she cried out with his every ramming motion, matching his roughness with her own wild fervency. The first warning he had was the sudden quivering of the round little belly against him and then she fell back, lifted violently, pushed harder against him as he lunged into her with all his force. She came then, her legs digging like soft vises into his sides, and her scream was muffled against his chest, a half-roar, half-gasp that seemed to pull every ounce of energy from her.

When it ended, she held a fraction longer against him to feel the magnificent contractions still inside her, and then she seemed to almost collapse beneath him. He slid from her, realizing with some surprise that he felt drained, too. He lay beside her, taking in the compact loveliness of her, an aggressive, determined little body, a tremendous driving power under the covering of the alabaster skin and fragile blondness. Deceptive, he thought, all the way through . . . a lovely deception, though.

She stirred, pulled herself up on her elbows, then to a sitting position, ran her hands down his muscled frame, caressing the maleness of him, then bending over to kiss him, a long, open-mouth kiss.

She pulled back finally, the high round breasts rising as she drew a deep sigh. He reached up with his hand, began to slowly circle each flat tip, then, with his tongue, tracing tiny paths around the very pink circles.

"Oh, God," she whispered, and the compact little body was lifting again.

"I didn't get to pay enough attention to these last time," he murmured.

"Yes, yes . . . oh, my God, yes," she groaned, and her legs moved up and down as he continued to suck each breast with gentle fervor. Her little cries became harsh ones and her body began its pumping and she pulled at him and once again there was the terrible desire for harsh, wild lovemaking. He impelled himself into her, again and again, and she screamed with pleasure until the last scream came once more against his chest.

When he fell, to lay beside her, he heard the sound of his own breathing mingling with her drawn gasps. Finally she turned to him, her china-blue eyes darkened as she gazed at him, as though she were trying to come to grips with herself.

"Stored dynamite," Fargo remarked. "It's got to explode."

"You sorry?" she asked with a quick edge.

"No, just wondering why you've stored it up for so long," he said.

"I told you, I wanted a man that wasn't afraid of me," she answered.

"You're going to have to settle for one of those gentlemen sooner or later," he told her.

"Maybe not. I've kept thinking a man will come along. I was right," she said.

He allowed her a chiding smile. "You know I wouldn't be part of your circle," he said. "Besides, I'm not the staying kind. You know that, too."

"Not for now you're not," she said.

"Meaning what?" he asked.

"Meaning maybe you'll come back," she answered. "Maybe I can make it so you'll not be able to forget me, so you'll spend all your time remembering."

He felt his lips purse. It was a new approach. "Maybe," he allowed.

"I'd say I made a good start," she said with a hint of smugness.

His smile said that he didn't disagree. He swung to the edge of the bed, started to reach for his clothes. "Stay, Dean's not due till morning," she said.

He held back the answer that leaped to his lips, decided the less said the better. "He could get in early," he told her, and pulled on trousers. He put his shirt over one arm and she rose from the bed, pressed herself against his chest, soft warmth and smooth skin.

"Why were you so sure?" she murmured. "You said you'd tell me."

There was the hint of a pout in her voice that made him smile at her. "It's sort of like when you're following a trail," he said, and saw her frown back at him. "You watch, you see, you listen, you smell, but that's not enough. You've got to become like the wild creatures, I guess the way men once were a long time ago. You have to learn to feel, to sense, to pick up what you can't see, hear, or smell, the way the field mouse knows danger before he sees or smells the fox, the way the lamb knows danger before he sees or hears the wolf. Teasing is teasing, words are just words. But I can feel the wanting in a woman, no matter what she says, if it's there." He paused, half-smiled. "It was there," he finished.

She pressed her lips to his. "Till morning," she murmured, closed the door softly after him.

He hurried down the dim corridor to his room, slept soundly until the morning sun woke him. He'd just finished dressing when Janet appeared at his door, a yellow blouse matching her blond hair, a high-necked white collar clinging to the alabaster skin of her neck. Spun sugar, he thought, half-laughed to himself.

"Dean's waiting downstairs. We both want to hear your report," she said. She made no reference to the night, her tone crisp, businesslike, as he started to follow her down to what passed as a dining room in the hotel. He rubbed his hand across her rear just before they reached the bottom of the stairs, received a glare of surprise.

"I liked it better last night, not so stiff-backed," he remarked blandly. She didn't reply, marched on ahead of him. He saw Dean Thornbury waiting at a side table and all the unanswered questions leaped inside him as he sat down across from the man. Dean greeted him with a smoothly pleasant smile. "Meet with your contacts?" Fargo asked as an elderly waiter brought him a cup of black coffee.

Dean Thornbury nodded, let a hint of disappointment touch his face. "Not all that successfully, I'm afraid," he said. "They seem to be having their hands full just existing. Handling anything more didn't get much response this time."

"Perhaps they'll feel differently if they were sure of a steady supply of goods," Janet offered.

"They won't be getting that," Fargo said sharply, quickly told them the harsh facts as he saw them about the Owl River Basin.

"Rather a discouraging report," Dean said when he'd finished.

"Just the truth of it," Fargo said.

"We'll have to pay attention to that," Dean Thornbury said. "But you mentioned one trail that might be usable for the good-weather months."

"Along a bur-oak rise," Fargo said.

"I'd like you to give us a finished trail map on that," Dean said. "While you're doing that, I'll follow up on some other contacts someplace else."

"That could take three or four days' work," Fargo said.

"That's all right. When you're finished, Janet will fill you in on where I'll want you next," the man said.

Fargo nodded, sipped his coffee. The assignment to fully trail-map the bur-oak rise could be a legitimate, honest desire on Dean Thornbury's part. It could also be a way to keep him busy and out of the way while he prepared his next move. Possibilities again, all guesses and conjectures, he reflected. He leaned back, raised the coffeecup to his lips. "I hear the slave hunter hit again yesterday," he said mildly, but his eyes were sharp on Dean Thornbury over the rim of the coffeecup.

"That's what I heard," Dean said.

Fargo searched his face for a telltale sign, a flicker, a moment's fleeting expression, a hint in the eyes. But there was nothing as Dean Thornbury let a completely open reaction mask anything else.

"You don't expect me to be upset over it, do you?" Dean asked.

"No," Fargo allowed.

"Hell, you know where I stand in the matter. He's doing a damn good job for us, whoever he is. The percentage of attempted runaways has dropped for everyone in the association. We're all happy as hell about what he's doing," Dean said. The man's openness was disarming, but openness could be the best of covers, Fargo reminded himself as he thought about red clay and expert marksmanship.

"Janet will stay on here to get your finished trail map," Dean said, rose, kissed his sister on the cheek, and Fargo's eyes followed the man from the room, his thoughts turning with the unresolved questions. He felt Janet's glance and turned to meet her tiny smile, more in the china-blue eyes than on her lips.

"Tonight," she said. "I'll be waiting."

"Tonight? Hell, I won't be half-finished," he told her.

"Did I say anything about maps?" she asked. "Or aren't you interested in coming back?"

He returned her narrow-eyed glance. "I'm interested," he conceded.

"Tonight, tomorrow night, the night after," she said.

"It'll take me twice as long to finish the mapping that way," he said.

The little smile came to her lips. "Yes, won't it?" she said.

He peered at her as the thought rose inside him for a moment. If the object was to keep him occupied, this would add to it. Was Janet a part of it, aiding her brother in his dual role? Fargo dismissed the thought. Any diversion in Janet Thornbury's mind was strictly her own, the light in her eyes attesting to that. Still, curiosity pushing him, he nudged at her. "How do you stand on the slave hunter and all of it? With your father and brother and the others?" he asked.

"No," she said without hesitation. "I don't go along with them on a lot of things. Why?"

"I did in two of the slave hunter's hired guns yesterday," he told her, saw her study his face for a long moment.

"I thought you weren't going to get involved in this whole business?" she said.

"I'm not. I only want to see Joseph Todd left alive. I told you that," he answered.

"He's Amity Sawyer's problem," Janet said, and he

watched the concern come into her eyes as she stepped closer, put both hands on his chest. "Stay out of it. You've helped her enough. It'll all pass one day and I want you alive then."

"Alive and remembering?" He grinned.

"Yes, full of remembering," she said.

He kissed her, a quick kiss, stepped back as her hands began to tighten on his shirt. "I'd best get moving if I'm coming back here tonight," he said, he said, and saw the pleasure of anticipation touch her round face. He strode from the hotel and ten minutes later he was saddled up and riding into the center of the Owl River Basin. She'd given him a sideways answer to his question, but it was enough. He couldn't expect a lot more, he reflected. She had been raised with a certain kind of thinking, a way of life and all the comforts that went with it. It was etched inside her, part of her very being, just as she was a product of that way of life.

Yet if she had come to second thoughts about it all, if she'd come to new understandings of her own, she could only be torn apart inside. If that were true, she had to be living in a world of inner conflicts maybe beyond her resolution. One didn't just wipe away a heritage, family loyalties, a way of life. He wondered if she were marking time, waiting for solutions to come from somewhere else. Something seethed inside her. He'd found out that much. The cotton-candy outside cloaked a little dynamo.

The bur-oak ridge rose up before him and he put aside further thinking about Janet Thornbury to begin making a trail map. He used his little notepad. Later he'd work from it on a larger sheet. He rode the beginnings of the trail, noting down turns, twists, streams, marking off natural guideposts, two large boulders facing each other, a twisted oak, a line of charred trees, a sudden cluster of pale-barked cottonwoods. He worked quickly, having decided to make it a rough map. There was damn little chance it'd ever be used anyway, and he wasn't about to let himself be kept out here.

Near the end of the day he spied a line of Indians, Pawnee, he guessed from the way they rode decorated saddle blankets. But no war party, squaws and kids with travois following the braves. He continued with his work until the light of the day began to fade and he turned the pinto, started back for Owl Bend.

It was dark when he reached the town. He stabled the pinto, went to his room, and washed the trail dust off. He put just trousers and shirt back on, sticking the Colt inside his belt, heard her come to the door at his knock. She had the kerosene lamp barely on, a flickering light suffusing the room. She wore the same frilly-collared nightdress, but this time she pulled the ribbon loose at the neck, let it fall open to show the high, very white twin mounds. Fargo put the Colt atop the dresser, started to reach for his belt.

"No, let me," she murmured, her eyes glowing darkly. Her hands opened the belt buckle, then his trousers, slid the legs down, and he heard her gasp, surprise and excitement mingling in the sound. "You've nothing on underneath," she murmured, let herself slide down to her knees, wriggled free of the nightdress. She clasped him to her, her face against his groin, laying his maleness against her cheek, rubbing, pressing, caressing.

"Oh, oooh, oh, yes . . . aaaah," the murmured little words coming from her as she continued to press and rub, and then he felt the soft wetness close around him. "Aaaaiiiii . . ." she gasped as she reveled in taking him to her. She moved back to the bed, lay down, her lips still around him, and now she was making tiny moaning sounds and her convex little belly pressed tight against him as he felt the little spasms run through her. They suddenly grew stronger and her mouth fell open, her

71

head arching back. "Oh, God, I'm going to come, oh, God," she half-screamed.

He thrust into her at once and she pumped back instantly, the frantic driving of her again overwhelming, and she managed to hold back the moment for a last few thrusts of ecstasy, and then she exploded with him, her scream pressed into his collarbone. She continued to pump after the supreme moment had gone, a reflex kind of action, unable to bring herself to a halt. From her little cries she seemed to enjoy the aftermath as much until finally she tapered off and lay quietly beneath him.

He tried to move from her, but her hands tightened, clutched him to stay, and he let himself rest inside the warmth of her. She stayed unmoving, holding him in place, and then, slowly, he felt her hips begin to move, a slow lifting, then a half-turn. She tightened around him and he felt himself respond, and as he did, the cry came from her, a whispered, sweet sound of pure awesome pleasure. "Uuuuuooooo . . . so nice . . . ooooh . . . yes," she murmured as she felt his response. Her lovemaking was no less driving this time; it only started slower, but it ended with her feverish pumping abandon and finally she lay beside him, completely spent. He was closing his eyes when he felt her turn to come against him, heard her voice whispering against his cheek.

"Good enough for remembering?"

"Good enough," he admitted, opened his eyes to see china-blue eyes watching him, her short blond hair and round face matching the compactness of her body, and he saw the tiny smug smile cross her lips. She closed her eyes and was asleep in moments.

She was still asleep when he left in the morning, and as he rode the pinto into the new sun, he found himself thinking about Janet Thornbury. Chances were he'd not come back to her any more than he had to any of the others, not while he still searched and hunted for that fi-

72

nal moment of justice. Yet he'd not easily forget her. She'd already made that a certainty and maybe she'd manage to do more before it was time to go. He laughed wryly. There was something very different about her than any woman he'd ever known. Not just the eagerness. He'd known enough eager women. Not the passion, either. Hell, he'd known more than enough passionate ones. Not just female possessiveness, either, something more than that, a kind of assured expectancy. It grew out of that inner drive that was hers, a quality impossible to precisely pin down, but it was more than simple self-confidence. He wondered if anyone had ever really said no to her. There was always a first time, he mused. But he wasn't ready for that yet, not with all that wanting waiting to explode for him.

He reached the bur-oak ridge, finished all the notes he'd need by early afternoon, and found a flat rock where he could spread out a square of paper. With a quill pen and a stoppered horn bottle he kept in the bottom of one of the saddle pouches, he drew a trail map on the square of paper, all the markings put down properly. He finished and let it dry in the last rays of the afternoon sun, folded it, and put it into the saddle pouch. It would stay there for another day. He had decided to let Janet think he'd another day's work to finish it. He'd dismissed the idea of her being in league with Dean, but if she knew he had finished, she'd have him stay and he wanted to pay Amity Sawyer another visit. Having another day's work left would give him both the excuse and the time to ride to Hillsville.

It was dark when he reached Owl Bend. Janet was waiting, no frilly-collared nightdress this time, only a sheet half wound around her that fell away a few moments after he stepped into the room. The driving wanting of her swept him along again, a wonderful, exhilarating trip as once more she exploded beneath him,

73

on top of him, and beside him until finally she lay limply, her breath shallow. There was no talk of remembering. There was no need for it.

Later, she pulled herself onto her elbows, her round face serious, the short blond hair a little yellow cap. "I won't be here tomorrow night," she said. He let his eyes question. "I'll be at Clayberg, in Goosefoot Valley," she said. "Dean will meet me there. I got a message. You'll be surveying Goosefoot Valley next."

Fargo frowned. Goosefoot Valley lay a good distance east of Hillsville, a long depression in the shadow of the Powhattie hills that ran far north. "Your brother picks a lot of wild places for his contacts," Fargo commented.

"We both pick them," Janet said. "The idea is to open new territories. I've an aunt who lives near there. I'll have to spend one day with her, but only one. The rest of the nights can be ours."

"That'd depend where Dean has me chasing trails, wouldn't it?" he asked.

He saw her face grow troubled and her lips pursed as she thought. "Yes, I suppose so," she murmured, and then, brightening, "I'll figure out something." She lay down against him. "You're habit-forming, you know," she said.

"Same to you." He laughed, took her in his arms to sleep.

He left with the morning and she seemed hard asleep, but as he closed the door behind him, he heard her murmur. "Hurry, I'll be waiting." The whisper followed as he went down the hallway.

He rode into the Owl River Basin a little while later, found a spring of fresh water, bathed, stretched out beside it, and let the sun dry and warm his nakedness. He dressed again, leisurely, found a cluster of fresh, tart gooseberries, and shared breakfast with a pair of thrushes. He glimpsed a line of bronzed-skin riders in the distance, too far away to discern tribal markings, watched them move in single file down a ridge and vanish. He cleaned the pinto's hooves and then, casting an eye skyward, he saw that the sun was starting to center itself for the noon sky. He swung onto the horse and turned back for the ride to Amity Sawyer.

It was almost dark when he passed Hillsville and went on to the Sawyer place. Jimmy was the first to see him, rushed from the house with his arm waving wildly. "Welcome back, Mr. Fargo," the boy called out, took hold of the pinto's bridle. "Can I unsaddle him for you?"

"Don't know that I'll be staying, Jimmy," he said, and saw the disappointment flood the boy's face. Joseph appeared, nodded his curly gray head graciously.

"Welcome indeed, sir," Joseph Todd said. "You will stay for a bite of supper at least, I hope."

"Maybe we'd best see that Amity's mind is on having a dinner guest," Fargo said. "But I thank you for the thought."

Joseph's smile was made of experience and wisdom. "You've come to understand her mighty quick, I'd say, Mr. Fargo," he remarked.

"Some," Fargo conceded. "Folks that carry things hard inside tend to get thorny outside."

The old man smiled again, nodded. "Indeed. She's been in a fearsome dark mood ever since Clarabelle Moore," he said.

The creak of the front door opening made Fargo turn, and he saw Amity appear, a beige dress that matched her hazel eyes clung to her somewhat angular shape and curled around the full undersides of her long breasts. Unsmiling, her eyes fastened on him and her voice carried more than a hint of hostility. "What are you doing here?" she slid out at him.

"I told you I'd be in touch," he said.

"So you did. The Thornburys give you a day off?" she said tartly.

"I came here to talk," he said, ignoring her barb.

"Your employers would fire you if they knew you were here, I'll bet," she said, her voice full of churlishness.

He held his temper. "Maybe, but I do what I want with my time," he answered.

"Not when you work for the Thornburys. They believe in owning people, or did you forget about that?" she flung back.

Joseph and the boy had discreetly slipped into the house, he saw, and his eyes turned into blue quartz and this time his voice held a knife-blade's edge. "Get the goddamn nettles out of your ass," he snapped. "Try to live up to your name. I didn't come here to listen to your sharp tongue. I came because I'm still trying to help you get Joseph to safety."

He saw her mouth tighten, but she blinked and he caught the angry pain in the hazel eyes. "Getting the slave hunter is the only help we need and you can't do that any more than anyone else," she said, but there was more resignation than anger in her tone now.

"Maybe and maybe not. It's getting Joseph to safety that matters to me. You said yourself maybe he'd be the exception," he reminded her.

"I know what I said," Amity snapped. "I was hoping and hoping's not enough anymore. Wishing's not enough, not with him out there."

Fargo saw the despair in her face, but she wiped it away as Joseph appeared in the doorway.

"Supper's ready, Miss Amity," he said, let a meaningful pause hang.

Amity's eyes met Fargo's half-amused stare. "You might as well sup with us," she said, turned, held the door open for him.

"I've questions," he said.

"After we've finished eating," she answered, and he followed her into a room where the table was set with dishes and a big crock, plates over the polished hardwood surface. Jimmy was already in his seat and Fargo took a chair across from Amity. Joseph brought him a bourbon and Fargo smiled his appreciation.

"Are you staying, Mr. Fargo?" Jimmy asked. "Can I unsaddle the pinto after dinner and rub him down? I've never rubbed down a horse like that."

Fargo's smile stayed in his eyes as he looked across at Amity. "Can't say for sure, Jimmy. It's been a long ride, though," he said evenly.

"Fargo and I will be talking a spell, enough time for you to rub down the Ovaro," Amity said, and Fargo smiled at the answer which said everything and nothing. He put his attention to the meal, simple but filling fare, boiled potatoes and slices of beef cooked long enough to take any toughness out of it, and it turned out that Amity had a fine hand for baking barmbrack bread and he helped himself to four of the fine-tasting slices. When the meal ended, Jimmy hurried outside to enjoy rubbing down the pinto and Fargo followed Amity into the living room. She turned, hazel eyes boring into him.

"First things first. You can stay the night, but that's all there'll be to it," she said.

"Of course. I didn't come expecting," he said mildly.

"*Hah!*" she snorted. "You always come expecting, Skye Fargo. Or hoping. It's built into you."

"You misjudge me," he said. Her expression was absolute disagreement. Her eyes studied him for a moment and he caught a question flickering behind the hazel orbs. "Go on, ask it, whatever it is," he tossed at her.

"I was just wondering if you see much of Janet Thornbury in your working for them," she said a shade too offhandedly.

77

"Some," he said evenly. "I still say she's not like the others."

Amity's disagreement was plain in the way her lips set tightly. "You said you had questions," she remarked.

"When do you try another run?" Fargo asked.

"The day after tomorrow. We'll be taking Henry Jones, a good man who ran away from the Ferrulls. He has family in Illinois," she said.

"How will you be going?" Fargo asked. "I'll try to ride backup if I can."

"North, through Goosefoot Valley, along the river," Amity said. He knew that surprise and alarm flashed across his face, and she picked it up at once, frowning at him. "What is it?" she asked.

"Why that way?" he asked.

"It's been planned. It's a fast route, straight north almost," she answered. "What's wrong?"

He thought for a moment. "I can't say anything is for sure, but Dean Thornbury is going to be riding in Goosefoot Valley," Fargo told her. She waited, her eyes still frowning at him. "He was in the Owl River Basin, too," Fargo finished.

Amity's frown deepened and he saw the thoughts racing behind her stare. "You think he's the slave hunter?" she questioned.

"I don't think anything yet. I'm just telling you the facts. And I was told that he's a crack shot," Fargo added.

Amity continued to frown into space. "Dean Thornbury," she said slowly, thinking aloud. "I guess it could be him as well as any of the others. Strange, though, I always thought it'd be someone they hired."

"I've no proof of it, just little bits and pieces," Fargo said. "But go another way. Play it safe."

"We can't, not this late. Everything's all set up. It can't be changed. There'll be others meeting us at St.

78

Joseph, across the Missouri line. There's no way to change it now," she answered. "And you say you've no real proof, anyway."

"That's true enough," Fargo admitted.

"In any case, he won't be breaking through this time," Amity added. "We're taking six extra riders, six more guns and six pair of extra eyes, that'll mean."

Fargo made no reply, unwilling to chip at her anxious optimism. From what he had learned so far, it'd take more than extra riders to turn away the slave hunter, and he wished he had more than bits and pieces to go on. "When will you start through the valley?" he asked.

"Late afternoon," she said. "That'll give the Missouri riders the night to travel."

"Late afternoon," Fargo echoed, his eyes narrowed in thought. It gave him time to be there, he pondered as Jimmy returned, his young face full of shining.

"Finished. It's sure nice rubbing down a horse like that one," the boy said.

Fargo fished into his pocket, found a silver coin, and tossed it to him. "Honest work deserves honest pay," he said, and Jimmy ran off happily to find Joseph.

Amity made a sharp sound. "Strange words, coming from some folks," she sniffed.

"Don't get your damn nettles out again," Fargo growled.

She cast him a stiff glance. "You'll be using the same room. I'm going to turn in now. Good night," she said, started to walk away with the abruptness of her words.

Fargo watched the beige dress moving with her long thighs, resting over hips that were all angles. Yet she moved with the easy grace he remembered, a sway to her walk that sent her long brown hair moving gently from side to side.

"Sleep well," he called. She didn't look back, didn't acknowledge the remark with even a pause in her steps as she disappeared around the corner of the doorway. Fargo smiled, again aware of how Amity Sawyer could throw both attractiveness and thorniness in unexpected ways, sudden bursts of either that took one off guard. And the streak of stubbornness was deep through her. He picked up his saddlebag and went to the small guest room, left the lamp out, and undressed to lay across the bed. A shaft of moonlight slid through the window to paint itself across his body.

He refused to let himself think about Dean Thornbury and the slave hunter. He'd nothing more to help make a firm connection. There was little he could do but wait and try to find more pieces, additional links. If there were any, he reflected. But he would be at the valley when Amity and the others made another run for it. He'd find a way to be there, he knew, and he swore silently at himself. No involvement, yet a damnsight more than curiosity. The conscience makes promises and then insists the flesh carry them out. "Damn," he swore. He was still glowering into space when he heard the door open, no quietness this time, and he watched as Amity appeared. She came into the room, barefoot but with a brown robe wrapped tightly around her, kept her eyes on his face.

"You can wipe that look away," she snapped. "I've some questions now."

"At this hour?" he asked mildly.

"Exactly. I was thinking and they kept poking at me. I want them answered so's I can sleep," she said.

"Out with them," he snapped, not moving from his position across the bed.

"If you found out that Dean Thornbury was the slave hunter, what would you do?" she asked.

Fargo found a thin smile. "Still trying, aren't you?"

"What do you mean?" she asked.

"You know damn well what I mean. You're still trying to box me into taking sides."

"I'm just asking a question," she demurred.

"Bullshit," he snapped.

Her lips bit into each other. "Well, would you or wouldn't you?" she pressed.

Fargo rose up on one elbow, stared into space for a moment. "I wouldn't have to do any deciding, not the kind you mean," he told her.

"Why not?" she frowned.

"If I found out, he'd sure as hell know about it. From there, I'd have no deciding to do. It'd all come down to staying alive, not to taking sides." He paused for a moment. "Maybe, in the end, the big words and fancy ideas all just come down to that when the chips are down." He met Amity's eyes again. "In this case, you can be damn sure that's what it'd come down to, with Dean Thornbury or anybody else it might be."

Amity's face stayed grave and he saw her deciding about his answer. "I guess so," she conceded. "Maybe you wriggled off the hook, but I guess you're right."

"You know I'm right, Amity," he said sternly.

"Good night, Fargo," she said, ending the exchange with definiteness. She turned to the door.

"Not going to stay?" he called to her.

She paused, fastened a hard glance at him. "No. Surprised, aren't you?" she said.

"A little," he admitted.

"Good," she snapped, closed the door after her, but he knew she had to hear his laugh.

He turned on his side and was asleep in minutes. He slept soundly, woke with the morning. When he'd dressed, he went into the living room and saw Amity had coffee ready. She handed him a steaming cup. She had her brown hair pulled back severely, but her shirt, opened low at the neckline, allowed just a glimpse of the line of her long breasts.

"You look tired. Have trouble sleeping?" he slid at her.

"Go to hell," she murmured as she poured coffee for herself.

"Stubborn can be stupid," he said smiling, as he sipped his coffee.

"Maybe," she conceded. "I call it principles."

"Such as?"

"Next time. You'll come wanting instead of expecting," she said.

"I will?" he asked in some surprise.

"Yes," she said, almost smugly. "Being near Janet Thornbury will make you come back wanting. It's known that she's a real tease. She likes to wave it in front of a man and then laugh at him. A real little bitch, I've heard. I'll wager she's waved it in front of you already."

"You could say that," Fargo answered blandly.

Amity continued to look pleased with herself. "You'll come wanting next time," she sniffed.

Jimmy came in, bursting with young energy. "I'll help you saddle up, Mr. Fargo," he announced, and Fargo rose, finished his coffee, and left with the boy, tossing Amity a smile that made her frown back. She was watching from the door as he rode out, and he halted for a moment.

"No promises, but I'll try," he said.

She nodded gravely. "Can't ask more," she said. "I guess."

"Damn, you're a thorn-tongued package, Amity Sawyer," Fargo growled, and she looked back at him with a silent acknowledgment that made her face pridefully lovely. He slapped the pinto's rump and went off in a fast canter, still muttering at her.

He rode east, skirted Hillsville, crossed into the rolling

82

land, continued to ride, detoured to avoid a distant line of single-file riders. He paused in midmorning to water the horse and munch on a bush of wild plums, and it was just into the early afternoon when he reached Clayberg, Goosefoot Valley lying behind it in the distance, looking like a long, wide funnel. He rode into Clayberg, a town distinguished by the bank being part of the dance hall. He'd dismounted and let the pinto drink at the water trough when he saw the tall, spare figure, the gray eyes hard, walking his horse along the street. The man espied him at the same instant, his smile thin.

"You look surprised, Fargo," Sam Tracy commented.

"Guess so," Fargo agreed with annoyance at himself. "Sort of out of your territory, aren't you?"

"Been chasing a rotten horse thief. Tracked him this far, then lost him. Got to pick up his trail again," the sheriff said.

"You alone?" Fargo asked casually.

Sam Tracy nodded. "Ned's back in Hillsville. Somebody's got to mind the store."

"Of course," Fargo said as a host of new thoughts poured through his mind. The pieces had all been shifted suddenly, new ones added, unanswered questions taking on few faces. He set them all aside for the moment, but he couldn't set aside the heightened feeling of new danger inside him.

"Saw Dean Thornbury," Sam Tracy said. "You're going to be trail-mapping in Goosefoot Valley, I hear." It was Fargo's turn to nod. "Maybe I'll run into you there." Sam Tracy smiled.

"You going into the valley?" Fargo returned.

"I figure that's where my boy has headed," the sheriff said. "We'll see," he finished, nodded again, and walked on.

Fargo pulled the pinto's head up, turned him from the water trough, and moved toward the white frame building with the battered sign over the entranceway that read CLAYBERG HOTEL. Dean appeared at the front steps as Fargo looped the reins around a hitching post. The man's face wore impatience, his mouth a thin line.

"Glad you're here. I've been waiting," he said.

"I've that trail map of the bur-oak rise for you," Fargo said, pulling the square of paper from the saddle pouch. Dean Thornbury took it, pushed it into the pocket of his jacket without a glance. Fargo felt a grim smile inside himself.

"Let's go inside. I'll go over things here with you quickly. I want to be on my way," Dean said.

"What's the rush?" Fargo asked mildly.

"I've people to meet. I don't want to keep them waiting for me to arrive," Dean said, and led the way to a round corner table in a worn foyer of the hotel. He had a crude map of the entire region spread out. "I want you to check out trails through the west slope here," he said, placing his finger on the outline of Goosefoot Valley. "That'd be the Bighorn range right there. Three families want to start a community up in that area."

"That's rough land up there," Fargo said as his eyes moved across the crude map. The Bighorn region of the west slope was all the way across Goosefoot Valley from the river. He picked words carefully. "Down by the river is a lot easier country," he remarked.

"Can't tell people where to set down," Dean Thornbury said a little peevishly. "Folks starting a new community need help. I promised them all I could give them."

"They sure will in that land," Fargo said.

Dean rolled up the crude map. "You just find me some good trails that'll take a wagon up there," he said. "I'll just get my things from my room and be on my way. You'll report back to Janet the way you did out of the Owl River Basin."

"Is she here?" Fargo asked.

"Yes, but she went out visiting. She'll be back late afternoon, I'd guess. She can fill you in on anything else. She went over everything with me yesterday."

"It'll be a good week before I've anything out of that rugged country," Fargo said.

"Janet'll wait in Clayberg for you," Dean said.

Dean started to stride off and once again Fargo chose words carefully, his voice casual. "You'll be in Goosefoot Valley looking for more folks settling down there, I take it," he slid out.

The man paused, glanced back at him. "Maybe, but then I'm thinking of going on to Sutter's Creek. Haven't decided yet. Why?"

Fargo shrugged. "Just curious." He smiled.

Dean Thornbury's mouth stayed a tight line, emphasizing the cruelty in it. "You just concentrate on the Bighorn area," he said, turned quickly, and strode off.

Fargo watched him climb the stairway to the second floor, waited but a few moments, and hurried outside to the pinto. He mounted the horse, rode with an easy trot through Clayberg, and moved from the town, heading west toward the long funnel that was Goosefoot Valley lying in the distance. But he turned from the road as he saw three serviceberry trees, heavily foliaged, their branches coming down low to the ground. He pushed his way through the thick, sawtoothed leaves until horse and rider vanished from sight. Sitting motionless, he peered through the curtain of foliage to the road some fifty yards away, completely invisible inside the trees to anyone on the road.

Travel in and out of Clayberg was light, he noted, a half-dozen riders moving into town, a fruit rack wagon with its low sides and removable racks, a girl driving a plum-colored buckboard and having trouble with a fractious, long-legged bay. Fargo continued to watch, a silent, unmoving figure. Only when he glimpsed the red roan riding from town did his eyes narrow. Dean Thornsbury sat the roan easily, a superior horseman's seat, Fargo took note, his eyes fastened on the man as he passed by. Horse and rider moved in a straight line, going on past a fork in the dry roadbed, and Fargo's lips edged a smile that was made of grim confirmation. Dean Thornbury had done his deciding and it was against going on to Sutter's Creek. Fargo made a small, harsh sound. If there'd ever been any real deciding to do, he reflected.

He set the question aside and returned his gaze to the road. Almost an hour went by before he saw the figure he waited to see, sitting very straight in the saddle, not as smooth a seat as Dean Thornbury. Fargo watched Sam Tracy's spare, unbending frame ride by, the man's face severe even at this distance. The sheriff continued straight along the road, moving his horse toward Goosefoot Valley. Fargo's eyes held for a moment on the big Winchester .44, the end of the barrel protruding from the rifle holster, the new front-end sights for long-range accuracy clearly visible. He watched until the sheriff disappeared down the road, then slowly moved the pinto from the leafy hiding place. He let thoughts revolve inside him as he started back toward town.

No answers, though, only more questions, he sniffed unhappily. Sam Tracy and Dean Thornbury, both headed into Goosefoot Valley, both with their glib reasons. Was one on his way to prepare for tomorrow? He turned the question in his mind. If so, it was only one. They weren't working together, he was convinced of that much. The slave hunter was a lone killer. Everything about his methods proved that. He believed in aloneness, trusted it, acted on it, took careful pains to ensure it. He'd hire faceless, expendable bodies and made certain they knew nothing of him. He knew the safety of loneness, Fargo reiterated silently.

But perhaps that careful construction would be torn down tomorrow, he told himself as he entered Clayberg. He stabled the pinto and returned to the hotel, sat down in the worn foyer, and watched the remainder of the afternoon drift into the gray purple of dusk. He forced himself not to think about either Sam Tracy or Dean Thornbury. There'd be time enough for that when tomorrow was over. He was sitting near the window and saw Janet as she came up the front steps of the entrance just as night fell, watched as she strode into the foyer. She wore a yellow skirt and a pink blouse that drew tight around the high, very round breasts. When she saw him, her eyes widened and she came to him at once as he stood up.

"Been waiting long?" she asked, the china-blue eyes concerned.

"Not too long," Fargo said. "Saw Dean earlier this afternoon. He's been gone some while now."

A tiny light flickered in her eyes. "Yes, I urged him to get an early start," she said. "Come with me. I want to get out of these clothes. I feel hot and grimy."

Fargo followed her to her room on the second floor, his glance taking in the spotlessness of her outfit. "Those clothes sure look bandbox fresh," he commented.

"Riding sidesaddle keeps them that way, but I feel like changing," she said as she opened the door of her room and he stepped inside with her. It was only then that she noticed he was carrying his saddlebag, watched him put it in a corner.

"You didn't get a room?" she said in surprise.

"Didn't see any need," he said blandly.

She stared back and he watched quiet amusement slide across her face. "I see," she commented. "The spirit of frugality?"

"The spirit of fucking," he said cheerfully.

Her eyes turned dark. The unvarnished honesty of his words seemed to explode inside her as she spun to him, one arm locking around his neck, the other tearing at her shirt. "Yes, damn you, oh, God, yes," she murmured, pressed his hand across one soft, high round breast, and groaned. A feverish desire swept through her and she pressed her crotch against him, pulled him back to fall across the bed with her. The rest seemed almost a kind of race between her craving and his ability to satisfy her, the driving, pressing, wanting of her more than he'd ever seen before.

"Again," she breathed after the first time, "again." And the gasped word came once more after she exploded beneath him a second time. The evening passed in the overwhelming spell of her almost insatiable needs, but finally her alabaster compact form lay beside him, thoroughly spent, her round face under the cap of short yellow hair now placid, more than satisfied.

She opened her eyes as she felt him watching her, lifted a hand to encircle his neck. "See what one night without you does?" she said, smiling.

"It wasn't all that," he answered.

"No, it wasn't," she conceded almost ruefully.

"Something inside you," he said. "It churns, a small volcano." She didn't answer and her silence was enough. "Trying to store up for the rest of the week?" he asked.

"Something like that," she muttered. "I know you won't be able to get back here every night from the Bighorn range."

"That's right," Fargo said. "Dean said you picked it out with him."

"I couldn't help that," she answered crossly. "Business is business." She sat up, turned to press her flat-tipped breasts against him. "When can you get back?" she asked, suddenly all eagerness. "Don't make it a whole week."

"Maybe I can do it in a few days. I'll see," he told her, and she hugged herself to him and was asleep in seconds, the short-cropped blond hair nestled into the hollow of his shoulder.

She slept soundly, stayed asleep as he woke in the morning, quietly pulled on clothes. As he closed the door behind him, he heard her stir, murmur his name, but he hurried down the stairway. He wanted an early start and he retrieved the pinto from the stable, saddled up quickly, and rode out along the road, the long funnel of Goosefoot Valley lying in front of him. He went on and moved downward into the green of the valley where he could see the river winding along the far side. He turned the pinto and began to climb in the opposite direction.

He rode unhurriedly, but anyone watching would see him heading up toward the Bighorn region far across the valley, following instructions. That was the way he wanted it and he wondered if eyes were watching. It was more than possible. He had already seen the care, the attention to details, that were part of the slave hunter. He couldn't risk not following instructions, Fargo told himself, not without a sense of irritation. To do anything else would show that he had suspicions and he couldn't reveal that . . . not yet. He'd have to climb toward the Bighorn region. There was no other way to play it, and he sat back in the saddle with feigned casualness.

Time would have to be measured carefully later, allowing enough to circle back and down to the river road. Timing was vital. He wanted to be close to the fleeing wagon with its human cargo, but not too close, hanging back just far enough to see what the others wouldn't see. He guided the pinto through a path under a thick overhang of trees, took note of the position of the

89

sun when he emerged. He'd gone more than halfway to the Bighorn region and he slowed. Anyone watching would have turned back by now, satisfied that he was going on. Fargo glimpsed a line of blue-violet closed gentians, then, nearby, yellow flashes of fringed loosestrife. Water somewhere near, he reflected, pools or high marshland fed by underground springs. The ground was taking on softness. He felt it in the way the pinto was lifting his feet.

He had just turned the horse to make his way to firmer ground when he pitched forward, almost out of the saddle, grabbing hold of the saddle horn to save himself as the pinto went down on one foreleg. Fargo leaped from the saddle as he regained his balance, landed on the soft ground just as the pinto drew his left foreleg up. "Shit, a stinking sinkhole," Fargo swore aloud as he stared at the ground where the pinto's leg had broken through to form a hole where the edges continued to crumble in. He swore again as he surveyed the sinkhole, a hidden, preformed hole created by underground water. They often fell in all by themselves, always when something exerted pressure on the surface.

The pinto held the foreleg up and Fargo knelt down to it at once. "Goddamn," he muttered furiously as he examined, stroked, felt, probed with hands both sensitive and experienced. Nothing broken, but a scrape and a sprain, a fast-swelling one, he saw, the ligaments already puffing up under the skin. He let the pinto put the foreleg down and the horse rested only a fraction of weight on it.

Swearing softly, Fargo lifted his eyes, scanned the terrain. He watched a covey of red-eyed vireos swoop down behind a line of shadbush just as another cluster took flight. He got to his feet quickly, nodding in grim satisfaction, and led the pinto slowly through the shadbush. The horse followed, limping on three legs, only touching the ground with the swollen foreleg. Emerging on the other side of the bushes, Fargo saw the water only a few yards ahead, a clear, cold oval depression fed by the underground streams that plainly honeycombed the area.

Fargo led the pinto into the pond, just over the horse's knees to let the cold water swirl around the swollen leg tendons. The pinto put his sprained foreleg down in the water, glad for the soothing, refreshing coldness on the injured flesh. Fargo stroked the horse gently until the pinto relaxed in the pool waters, keeping his injured foreleg immersed. He moved onto the grass then, looked up at the sun, and swore silently. It would be midday soon and at least another four hours before the pinto could use the foreleg. "If then," he muttered angrily. It could be five hours. Pushing a lame horse would only make the injury turn worse. There was not a damn thing to do but wait till the swelling went down completely so the leg could take hard riding.

"Stinking shit luck," Fargo swore, and knew the feeling of utter frustration. He lay back on the grass, pushed his hat down over his face, and forced himself to lie quietly. Every half-hour he checked the pinto's leg and began to allow himself hope as the swelling started to go down.

When the horse stepped out of the cool water by himself, Fargo used an old shirt to soak and wrap it around the leg, keeping the area between the fetlock and the knee wet and cooling. And each time he checked the leg he took a bearing on the sun, watched it move across the sky. "Not so fast, dammit," he muttered upward at one point. But the sun continued its march across the sky and the afternoon inexorably moved toward an end. It was late afternoon when Fargo took the wet cloths from the foreleg for still another time. The swelling had gone down altogether, he saw, took the reins, and walked the horse back and forth, watching as the pinto put his full weight on the leg. Murmuring a small prayer, Fargo swung onto the pinto's back, let the horse move again as he peered down at the foreleg. The horse continued to use the leg normally.

"Let's go, dammit," Fargo said, and started the pinto back down the slope. The sky was slipping into gray purple, but he didn't press the pinto too hard, letting the horse move on his own, pick his own terrain so long as it went downhill. He came into sight of the river, then the narrow road running alongside it. When he reached the level ground, he pushed the pinto harder, broke the horse into a gallop. Amity and the wagon would be well on ahead by now, all his plans for perfect timing shot to hell. He kept the pinto galloping flat out alongside the riverbank.

The land rose up in a series of hills at his left as he raced on and he scanned the hills as he peered ahead for a glimpse of the wagon. The grayness was growing heavier as, rounding a turn in the road, he saw the men on the hills, most on foot, rifles in hand, a few on horseback. One peered down at him, recognized him from Owl River, and beckoned frantically to him. Fargo pushed the pinto up through thick, high brush covering the slope and the man called to him as he neared.

"We got him," the man cried out, his face flushed with excitement. "He's hiding in the brush somewhere."

Fargo glanced at the others as they moved quickly back and forth through the thick brush of the hillside. "You see him?" he asked.

"No, but we spotted his horse. Right there." The man pointed and Fargo followed his wave to where a black horse stood quietly under the branches of an oak. "We come racing up here the minute we spotted the horse. He didn't even have time to get a shot off at the wagon he was so busying ducking for cover. We'll find him this time."

Fargo's eyes were ice. "Where's the wagon?" he barked.

"Gone on," the man said.

"Shit," Fargo roared, wheeled the pinto in a tight circle, and started to race down the slope.

"Ain't you goin' to help us find him?" the man shouted, but Fargo was bent low in the saddle, his lips drawn back in a furious grimace. Back on the winding roadway, he sent the pinto flying forward, winced as he heard the foreleg pounding on the ground, but it seemed to be holding up. "Good leg," he muttered into the wind. He raced around a curve, peered ahead, saw only the empty road, swore, and pressed the pinto on. Another curve came up, sharper, and he leaned in the saddle as the pinto hurtled around it. He had almost rounded the curve when he heard the shot, the single, sharp crack of a high-powered rifle, an unmistakable sound.

"Aaaawww, goddamn," he groaned as the pinto came out of the curve. He saw the wagon, some hundred yards ahead, just about to go into another curve, but now the driver reining the horses to a halt. He was at it before the wheels stopped rolling, hurtling past it, his eyes sweeping the hillside as he turned the pinto and raced upward. The top of the hill was empty save for a tall white cedar, and he cursed inwardly as he reached the top, looked down at a back slope thick with dense tree cover. Fargo halted, his mouth a thin, bitter line. The slave hunter was gone, beyond catching. He saw where the man had raced into the trees, outer branch ends freshly broken off. But the killer had too much of a start and he was damn sure the man had mapped out the fastest pathways through the thick tree cover for himself. He could pick up the trail, follow, but catching

93

up to him was out of the question. It'd be all just wasted motion.

He turned the pinto, slowly rode down the hillside to where the wagon had halted. Amity and two other people, a man and a woman, sat stiffly inside the wagon where a piece of canvas covered the figure of Henry Jones. Amity's eyes found his, hazel circles full of defeat and pain as the other riders came racing up the road. "We heard the shot," the first one shouted as he reined to a halt and the others followed to gather silently around the wagon in a half-circle.

Fargo fastened them with a glare of bitter anger. "You damn fools," he flung at them. "Christ, how could you be so stupid?"

The men stared back at him, uneasy protest gathering in their eyes. "We thought we had him," one said.

Fargo swept the defense away with ice-cold, scathing words that became spears. "Sure you did. You thought he'd left his horse out in plain sight where you could spot it? How the hell could you think he'd be that dumb?" Fargo saw the slow realization begin to form in their eyes. "Oh, he left that black horse there, all right, but so you'd be sure and see it. He knew you'd do just what you did, leave the wagon and race up there to start beating the bushes. He threw out the bait and you bit at it."

Fargo turned away from their openmouthed frowns, the shocked realization stark in their eyes now. He focused on Amity as she sat alone on the wagon, arms clasped to herself. "I'm sorry. The pinto came up lame. I couldn't get here any sooner," he said. "Bad luck all around this time." She simply stared back at him. "I'll be in touch," he said, turning the pinto.

"Why?" he heard her almost whisper as he rode slowly on.

5

The reply rode with him as he turned the pinto upward, letting the horse slowly move toward the distant Bighorn region. It had come out of the pain and terrible bitterness inside her, he knew, and the corroding fear that Joseph would fare no better. Fargo found himself cursing the killer who called himself the slave hunter. He was not only clever and careful but this time he'd been lucky as well.

The night came to wrap itself around the valley, but Fargo continued climbing. He'd go on, with all of it, until he saw Joseph to safety or found out the answers to this murderous charade. But first he'd carefully sort out what little he had. So far he could still move freely. It was probable that Dean Thornbury didn't know he'd been at the attack at the Owl River Basin and just now the killer had vanished before he'd rounded the curve. The same held true for Sam Tracy. Fargo's eyes took on the color of blue shale as the horse continued its climb. Joseph Todd was next in line. He had to fit the pieces together before then. He had to be certain.

Fargo made camp just short of the Bighorn area, sat before a small fire, and leaned his broad back against the dark and grainy bark of a black oak. It was time to take stock, to put together whatever he had. There were new pieces. He had to fit them in. It was time to weigh, to evaluate, to make mental lists. He closed his eyes to help himself concentrate. He'd start with Sam Tracy.

One, the sheriff had been in the valley. Two, he could easily have been at the Owl River Basin. He carried a long-range Winchester and he was a crack shot. He had answers for his sudden appearance, for going into Goosefoot Valley. Reasonable answers. And convenient, glib ones. Sam Tracy had the freedom to roam, to give excuses to get away, to give himself plenty of time to pick and choose his spots and lay careful plans. The slave hunter needed time, to prepare, to switch horses, to map out escape routes, to have every part of his plans in order. Sam Tracy had the opportunity and the time for that. He fitted. Except for one point. Sam Tracy was no extraordinary horseman and the slave hunter could ride as well as he could shoot. A minor point compared with all the rest, Fargo speculated. He made mental note of it and set Sam Tracy aside.

He turned thoughts to Dean Thornbury. He had been in Owl River and now in the valley. He was supposedly an excellent shot and he was plainly an excellent horseman. Dean Thornbury had set up a pattern of movements that put him at the right place at the right time. Was the search for new business outlets all a clever deceit that let him be where he wanted to be at the right moment? Was it all an elaborate scheme that afforded a perfect cover, even to making his sister an unwitting part of it? Fargo thought of how Dean had pushed the trail map into his pocket without so much as a glance. Because it really didn't mean a thing to him? A minor point, yet little things often revealed a lot. He thought back to the questions he had had when the Thornburys first offered him the job. Had he been right from the very start? Was the job another careful move engineered by Dean, designed to keep him busy and safely away from helping Amity Sawyer. It certainly fitted, made of

96

the kind of careful planning and attention to detail that marked the slave hunter.

Fargo let his speculation move on, determined to examine every angle. What if it were someone else entirely, he deliberated. Henson. The man came to mind and he found himself rejecting the idea almost at once. Henson was full of wild rages, an undisciplined bully. He could never be the slave hunter. Temperament ruled out that. But what if it were entirely an outsider or a killer hired by the association from outside as Amity suspected? Fargo let the thought hang for a moment. He couldn't ignore the possibility. Hell, he couldn't dismiss anything yet, he answered angrily.

He thought about the question Sam Tracy had raised, a Judas among the free-staters. Even if the man had tossed the question out only as a clever bit of distraction, there could be more than a little truth in it. Somehow, someway, the slave hunter knew the times and routes used. Fargo felt the fire dying out, opened his eyes to stare into the last of the flickering bits of flame. His thoughts kept returning to Dean Thornbury and Sam Tracy. No outsider, he muttered to himself. One or the other. Everything pointed that way. But it was still all bits and pieces, nothing clear, nothing defined, nothing that could let him act. He needed more. He needed the proof that would change supposing to knowing.

Dammit, he needed more time, time to probe, to push, to let someone make a mistake. He'd have to convince Amity to wait, put off Joseph's flight. Fargo leaned forward, tossed a handful of dirt to snuff out the remains of the fire, and lay back for a weary but unsettled sleep.

He woke with the new day, checked the pinto's foreleg to see if it had swollen again during the night. Satisfied that the leg was back to normal, he set off for the Bighorn region. In his notepad he mapped out the few trails that offered any passage for a wagon, worked from dawn to dusk, did the same for the following two days. He finished on the third day, wanted to get back to Clayberg for more than one good reason, which included soft arms and warm lips, but other things had to come first and he headed away from Goosefoot Valley, across the top of the slope toward Hillsville and Amity Sawyer.

Night had come to cloak the land when he neared the house where a lone square of light reached from a window. Amity heard the horse halt as he dismounted and she came to the door with a rifle in her hand, Jimmy anxiously watching from inside the room.

"Just me," Fargo said as she peered out, the gun aimed steadily at him. He saw her lower the barrel after a moment.

"Little late to come calling," she remarked, but he knew the real meaning of the rifle was not the hour but fear.

"We have to talk," he said.

"Hi, Mr. Fargo," Jimmy called as Fargo stepped inside, ruffled the boy's hair.

"You were on your way to bed, Jimmy," Amity said, her face unsmiling as she set the rifle down.

"I'll be stopping back." Fargo smiled at the boy and Jimmy nodded, hurried from the room, and Fargo listened to his footsteps going down the dark hallway to the very end. He turned to Amity. She stood very straight, the long breasts pushing their pear-shaped bottoms tight against her dress, but the hazel eyes held only pain and turmoil. "I need more time," Fargo said curtly. "Hold off the run with Joseph."

"I don't control that. There's a schedule, others involved. You know that," she answered.

"Delay. The schedule's all shot to hell," he said.

She shrugged. "I don't know. It's a chain. There are others that have to be contacted. I don't know if I can."

"Where are you going to make the run?" he asked.

"Along Boulder Road, straight north till we near the corner of Missouri," she said.

"When?"

She shrugged again. "I'm waiting to hear. Soon, though, a matter of a few days, I'd guess."

"Put it off, make an excuse. I'm close, I tell you, close. I just need a little more time," he insisted.

The wounded eyes peered back. "You were close in the Owl River Basin, close in Goosefoot Valley. Close doesn't mean a damn."

"You've nothing to lose. Give me a chance to give Joseph a chance," he tossed at her.

"That's hitting low," she glowered.

He didn't answer as she wrestled with her own thoughts. "There's something else," he pushed at her. "He always knows where and when. You've a Judas sheep someplace."

Defensiveness touched her eyes. "Not here. We've talked about that. Not here, we're sure of that."

"Somebody at the other end?" he suggested.

"Possible, but we don't believe that. Getting everything together takes doing, wagons, horses, outriders, messages back and forth, everything all set up. There's no keeping it a real secret. Others listen, overhear, talk. Money buys information. Greed sells it."

Fargo shrugged. It wasn't important, not anymore. All that mattered now was proof, knowing the name, the face of a cold and calculating killer. He saw Amity's sidelong glance. "What if I delay a few days and you don't find out anything more?" she asked.

"I'll find out, dammit," he snapped, and wished he were as sure as he sounded. "I'll find out or I'll ride the run with you. I'll get Joseph through."

Her eyes stayed skeptical. "You thought it was Dean Thornbury. Change your mind?" she pressed.

"No, but thinking isn't enough. I've got to know. That's why I need more time," he answered.

She wanted to hope. He saw it in her eyes, but despair was a suffocating blanket and she paused again before answering. "I'll try. I don't know if I can, but I'll try," she said. "I can tell you in a day or so," she said almost resignedly.

"I'll get back." He nodded and her eyes followed him as he went to the door. His hand was on the doorknob when he heard her call, her voice flat.

"Stay," she said.

"Meaning what?" he asked.

"Sleep beside me. Nothing more, just that. Lay beside me," she answered.

"You trusting it'll be nothing more?" he said.

"Trusting and knowing," she said. "Just the way you know."

"Why?" he asked, suddenly curious.

"I'm tired of feeling alone," she answered, her voice still flat.

He searched the hazel eyes. No coy games, no masks, only a terrible weariness, and he understood, took his hand from the doorknob. She turned and he followed her into her bedroom along the other hall. He undressed beside her, lay down on the big bed, and felt the exhaustion wrap itself around his body at once. She came to lay beside him and he felt the bone of her angular hip. She turned, finally, pressed herself against him, the long, full-bottomed breasts resting against his ribs, her one hand on his chest. He heard the even breathing of sleep from her in minutes, settled down deeper into the bed and slept also in but minutes.

He slept heavily until just before dawn, waking with the inner clock he had long ago learned to set for himself. He slid from beside her, saw that she hadn't changed position at all, her long thighs a lovely line in the faint light starting to move into the room. He dressed silently, quickly, paused at the door to look back at her. She lay unmoving, her hand on the bed where it had lain upon his chest. Damn her, he murmured inwardly, making everyone in reach a partner in her own crusades and compassions.

He left, rode out as the sun began to touch the tops of the trees, crossed Goosefoot Valley, and reached Clayberg in the late afternoon. He found both Janet and Dean Thornbury sitting inside the hotel lobby, plainly waiting for him. Dean wore riding breeches and a white coat with a black string tie and looked the landed gentleman. But his face was sullen, his glance up at the big man one of annoyance.

Fargo shifted his eyes to Janet. She wore a pale-blue dress, fluffy at the collar, and the high, alabaster breasts demurely hidden, the outfit matching china-blue eyes. But in the round orbs, a very private anger blazed, at odds with the spun-sugar exterior.

"You're finally back," she remarked icily.

Fargo's gaze was bland. "Told you it'd take time," he said calmly as he eased his big frame into a small chair. The old man who doubled as porter and waiter came by and Fargo ordered a bourbon. "Found two or three trails that might do for you," he said, addressing Dean. "I'll set them down on a proper map tomorrow."

Dean Thornbury's face stayed at the edge of sullenness. "Janet and I were just talking about things. Most of my initial contacts aren't holding up," he said.

"You saying you don't need the trail maps?" Fargo frowned.

"Maybe not. But you'll be paid for your work, don't worry on that score," the man said crossly.

"I'm not," Fargo said, and the meaning hung clear in the two words. His bourbon arrived and he sat back,

sipped it, ignoring Janet and her brother. Janet responded quickly, as he expected.

"You seem preoccupied, Fargo," she remarked, and
the ice was still on her words.

"Guess so," he agreed, sipping his drink.

The irritation grew stronger in her tone. "May I ask
what about?" she pressed.

He waited a moment, let his glance rest casually on
her, then on Dean Thornbury. He had the words ready,
chosen on the long ride from Amity's. "Thinking about
Joseph Todd," he said. "I heard the slave hunter got another runaway."

"Yes, that's the only good news I've heard on this
trip," Dean said coldly.

"Now, Dean, you know Fargo's concerned about that
Joseph Todd," Janet soothed.

Dean Thornbury stood up, his face angry. "I don't
give a damn about Fargo's concern," he snapped, turning to the big black-haired man. "You know, you're not
being paid to worry about runaway slaves, Fargo. I sug-
gest you concentrate on those trails maps. I want them
first thing in the morning."

Fargo didn't answer, sipped his bourbon calmly, and
Dean Thornbury stalked off angrily. The man was a
good actor or he had something else in his craw, maybe
some of both, Fargo reflected. Janet's voice cut into his
thoughts to give him an unexpected answer.

"Please don't mind Dean. He's upset. He's been sitting
around for days trying to decide where to go next. Waiting and wondering always gets to Dean," she explained.

Fargo kept his face expressionless, drained the bourbon as his thoughts leaped. Dean Thornbury was waiting and wondering, but not about business. Word hadn't
come to him on the next run and he needed time to
prepare. His edginess was one more piece fitting into
place. Fargo felt Janet's hand touch his leg under the

table and suddenly her voice was husky, almost a whisper.

"Dammit, you were going to be here yesterday. Four days is too long. I stayed up waiting all last night," she breathed.

"Couldn't make it," he said. "And tonight I've got to draw up the trail maps. You heard your brother."

Her voice took on angry determination. "Draw fast because I'm not waiting another night," she murmured, and her china-blue eyes were dark-blue pools of insistence, her round face set with held-in desire, and the soft-blue frilly exterior was suddenly out of place.

"We'll see," Fargo said evenly.

"You're just being rotten," she said, and rose to swirl away, a softly moving blur of blue cotton candy.

Fargo smiled, got a room for himself, and brought up his saddlebag. He stripped down to just trousers, took out a square of paper, his notepad, and his stoppered ink bottle and quill. He began to draw the first of the maps from his notes. Night fell and he brought the little lamp to the table, continued working. He'd all but finished the last of the maps when he stopped, stoppered the bottle, and stretched out on the bed. He frowned up at the ceiling and his thoughts revolved, none of them about the maps. That was finished, for all intents and purposes, his mind going back to Amity.

She'd given no promises on being able to delay. Time was still all important. He couldn't wait for more pieces to fall into place, for a lucky break. He had to make things happen, find a way to force a mistake, break it into the open. He drew his lips back in distaste. He didn't like the idea, but there was no other way. He'd use Janet. She and Dean were close and he'd involved her in his elaborate cover. They talked, as brother and sister and as associates in the same venture. Fargo's eyes narrowed as he stared up at the ceiling, let his plans evolve almost of themselves. Nothing direct, not with Dean Thornbury. That's why he had to use Janet. He'd plant a seed, that's all he needed. If he did it right, it'd take root damn quickly.

Fargo still peered into space when the faint tap came at the door. He swung from the bed, opened the door, and Janet slipped in, a big, blue bathrobe all but hiding her. She let the robe fall away and she was naked beneath it, her high, round breasts pushing upward at him, her full, firm compact body quivering. Her lips moved, opened, no sound coming from them, and she flung herself at him, hands frantically pulling at his belt, pushing trousers down. Her mouth pressed into his chest, across his stomach, and he felt her slide downward, pressing her face into his thighs, across the deep denseness of his jet-black covering, and then the half-scream came from her, a cry of triumph, muffled at once, turning into little murmuring sounds of delight.

He moved to the bed with her and she refused to let go. He lay back, let her swing herself atop him. "Fargo, oh, Jesus, Fargo," he heard her cry, words, the first ones since she'd entered the room. But the words became only sounds again and he turned with her, tried to smother the feverish franticness in her with his body. Slowly he slid into the haven she pushed at him and her scream was more than pleasure, paradise rediscovered, and he closed his mouth around the alabaster breasts, moving from one to the other as she cried and moaned, urged, demanded, swept him along with the overwhelming wanting of her.

But finally the little room was still except for the harsh gasps of her breath as she lay limply beside him. He watched her not without a kind of awe. "You sure as hell store up fast," he said, enjoying the smooth roundness, the firm, compact loveliness of her body.

"Remembering," she breathed. "For me and for you."

"You're doing good at it," he admitted.

She half-turned, pulled herself up to lay across him, and he saw the hint of a pout turn her lips outward and the china-blue eyes took on a half-glower.

"What is it?" he asked.

"I keep wondering if you were out looking for signs of the slave hunter yesterday when you should have been here," she muttered.

"Would I do a thing like that?" he asked blandly.

"You damn well would," she snapped, and then, softening, "you and your sympathy for the old man."

"Maybe," he said. "It doesn't matter now anyway."

She peered at him. "Meaning what?"

"I think the slave hunter is going to miss out on Joseph Todd," Fargo said casually, but every word carefully weighed. "I know Amity Sawyer has different plans for Joseph. She won't be making the usual run for it. She'll just take off some night on her own with him, just she and Joseph, and there'll be no way for anyone to know or to get ready."

"Good," Janet sniffed, the half-pout still with her. "Then it'll be done with one way or the other."

"And I won't be concerning myself over it any longer, is that it?" Fargo laughed.

"Exactly," she snapped.

"That ought to make Dean happy, the way he barked about it this afternoon. Maybe you ought to tell him so's he can simmer down." Fargo grinned.

"I wasn't thinking about Dean," Janet said stiffly. "I was thinking about me, about us. That's all I've been thinking about these past four days." She slid arms around him, pressed the two wonderfully round mounds into his chest. "This'll all be over one day. I want you to come back, Fargo."

"Seems I heard that." He chuckled.

"I want it more than ever now. I knew we could do great things together," she said.

"I'd say the first thing now is for you to get the hell out of here unless you want to be running into people in the halls come morning," he said.

"No, I don't want that," she agreed, swung herself from the bed with a bouncing motion. She scooped up the big blue robe and disappeared inside it again, and he let her out with a pat on her rear, watched her hurry down the dim hallway. He returned to the bed, stretched out, held sleep off for another moment. The seed had been planted, given to her to carry, and he was sure she'd do so. He'd even given her a push in the right direction. He turned on his side, closed his eyes. There was nothing to do now but wait, the wheels set in motion.

He slept later than he'd intended, rose, and finished the last few touches on the maps, folded them together, and took them with him as he went downstairs to hunt up some breakfast. He managed to find coffee and a hard roll, then went to the stable where he paid the small fee to wash the pinto and give him a good currying until the black and white coat sparkled. When he finished, he strolled back to the hotel to see Dean on the front steps. "Been waiting for you," the man called. "Have you the maps?"

Fargo handed the folded squares of paper to him. "All done," he said.

Dean pushed them into his pocket. "I'll go over these carefully later," he said, and Fargo smiled inwardly. This time the man remembered to at least keep up pretenses. "I've got to pack up," Dean said, and Fargo let his brows lift in question. "Made some decisions this morning," Dean Thornbury said. "I'm going back home for a few days, maybe a week. Janet's going with me."

"Back home?" Fargo echoed.

"Yes, until I've set up some new plans," Dean said. "You get yourself a room in Hillsville and wait there till I'm ready for you." He turned abruptly, strode into the hotel, and Fargo watched him with narrowed eyes. Back home, he echoed silently. The seed had taken root to sprout even faster than he'd expected. Dean Thornbury was rushing back home and back home meant close to Amity Sawyer, close enough to be able to find a way to watch her, prepare, make plans. Another piece had fallen into place. Only one more to go and he'd be ready for that, he promised himself.

He started to go to get his gear when Janet appeared, looking taller in a leather riding skirt and a shirt to match her hair. "You heard?" she asked at once.

He nodded. "Sort of sudden, wasn't it?" he remarked.

"Maybe, but Dean's been upset at how things have gone, as you saw. He wants time to rethink the whole idea. Then he felt he'd left Daddy running things alone for long enough," she said. "We talked about it this morning and I agreed."

Fargo smiled back. "You tell him I'd not be concerning myself much more about Joseph Todd?" he asked.

"Yes." She frowned. "You as much as told me to. I didn't see anything wrong in that." She looked hurt at once.

"No, not at all. I'm just curious," he said soothingly, and her frown slid away. "How does all this leave us?" he asked.

"You'll be getting a room at the hotel in Hillsville, won't you?" she said, and he nodded. "Then it leaves us just fine," she said smugly, and he nodded understanding. She blew him a kiss as she left and he took the steps to his room. He sat down, waited, gave her time to leave with her brother, then got the pinto and slowly turned the horse back across Goosefoot Valley in the direction of Hillsville. He rode slowly, made a circle that brought him out west of Hillsville, and he moved up around the land near Amity Sawyer's house. No real high land, he observed, but plenty of ground cover. It wouldn't be hard to keep watch on Amity Sawyer's place, or have someone do it. Fargo scanned the terrain once more and then rode on to Hillsville. The town and the hotel were becoming familiar territory, he noted wryly as he stabled the pinto and got himself a room.

When he'd settled in and the night came, he decided to stroll down to the dance hall, a grubby little place duplicated in a thousand towns across the country. Only someone with a sense of humor had named this one the Royal Palace. It was a time for watching, asking questions, listening. Dance-hall girls and liquor made men talkative, quick to brag, gossip, and carry tales. Dance halls were also a good place to spot new faces. They stood out from the regulars in a dozen little ways. He had just reached the slatted, swinging door of the Royal Palace when he saw the tall, spare figure sauntering toward him.

"Back in town, are you?" the sheriff drawled.

"Boss's orders." Fargo smiled. "I see you're back, too."

"I work here, remember?" Sam Tracy said. "You were out Amity Sawyer's way," he remarked coolly.

Fargo knew that surprise touched his face. "Just passing by," he said.

"Keep it that way. I told you, I don't want trouble stirred up around here," Sam Tracy said, his voice even.

"You get around," Fargo commented.

"My deputy, Ned, spotted you out there," the sheriff said.

"He spend a lot of time watching Amity Sawyer's place?" Fargo questioned, not hiding the sharpness in his voice.

The man's face stayed expressionless. "I have him

make the rounds," he answered. "See you around, Fargo."

The tall figure sauntered on as Fargo's thoughts circled like a corralled mustang. Sam Tracy was full of convenient excuses again. Damn, Fargo swore softly. Was he concentrating on the wrong man? "By the way," he called out. "You catch your horse thief?"

Sam Tracy glanced back. "Nope. He got clean away," he said, and kept walking.

Nice and neat, Fargo contemplated in irritation. Everything all in place, convenient reasons followed by convenient answers. Damn, he swore again as he pushed open the swinging door and went into the dance hall. Dean Thornbury still fit the best, he muttered inwardly. He'd have answers soon enough. He sat down at a corner table that gave him a good view of the room, the long oak bar to one side, the round tables spreading across the floor with a tiny circle left for dancing, a gesture more than anything else.

He saw the girl come toward him at once, her practiced eyes moving over him with more than the stock display of interest. She wore a tight green-silk dress that barely contained oversized breasts. She was a big girl, wide hips, tall, a large frame, but still young enough to give her size a crude, overflowing sexuality. She slid into the chair beside him, her big breasts all but falling out of the low-necked dress. A shock of curly red hair out of a bottle topped a flat, aggressive face.

"Well, hello, big feller," she began. "I'm Crystal."

He tossed her a quick smile that held a kind of dismissal. "Sorry, Crystal, but I'm not your man tonight," he told her.

"Honey, I think you'd be my man any night," she said.

"Thanks, but not tonight," he said, and she gave a disappointed shrug that was not all performance. "But I'll pay for some talk," he said, and she gave a narrowed glance back.

"What do you want to know, big feller?" she asked.

"What makes you think I want to know anything?" He grinned at her.

"You're not the small-talk kind. You've got questions," she said.

"Maybe," he allowed. "Any new faces come in today?"

She shook the brassy red curls. "Just you," she said.

"Hear any talk about the one they call the slave hunter?" he asked idly.

He saw her draw into herself. "I don't get into that stuff," she said.

"You mean politics?"

"Taking sides, politics, ideas, you name it. That business can get a fight started around here real quick," she said.

"I didn't ask you for your opinions. But people talk to girls. You listen, you take it in. What've you heard?" Fargo pressed.

She lowered her voice. "Only that he hit again. Some folks like him, some don't, but nobody wants to tangle with him."

"Nothing more, nothing about another runaway?" he asked.

"No. Folks don't like talking about the slave hunter, no matter what side they're on. I think he scares them all," she said.

Fargo took the bills from his pocket and pressed them into her hand under the table. "I'm at the hotel. You see any new faces, hear anything worth telling, I want to know fast," he said.

"Sure. Thanks," she said, taking the bills from his hand as she rose.

He watched her leave, swinging her big frame with an easy grace that was as much natural as practiced. He had another bourbon, watched the dance hall grow more crowded, all customers who were plainly regulars. He finished his drink and started for the door when Henson and a handful of men entered. Henson wore the red dotted kerchief that seemed to be his trademark and Fargo recognized one of the others from that first day beneath the tree. Henson halted, stared hard at the big black-haired man.

"Look who's back," he sneered. "Mr. Busybody." He pushed his face forward. "I didn't forget how you helped that damned Sawyer girl and her old runaway," Henson growled.

"I always like to be remembered," Fargo said.

"She'll never get that runaway out alive," Henson said.

"Oh?" Fargo said, letting one eyebrow lift. Henson looked smug. "Who told you that? Your boss?" Fargo asked, keeping his voice casual.

"He didn't have to tell me that," Henson said, and drew bragging confidence around himself. "Somebody'll stop her. She won't get away with what she did. She won't run him off free."

"Somebody? You mean the slave hunter," Fargo said.

"Maybe," Henson returned, and Fargo saw the cunning slide across his face. Henson brushed past on his way to the bar, the others following close at his heels, and Fargo went outside, strolled back toward the hotel. Was Henson parroting something he'd heard, something Dean Thornbury had let drop, Fargo wondered. Or was he just spouting hot air? The man was a surly braggart, the kind that enjoyed sounding important.

Fargo reached the hotel without answers for himself, went up to his room. His hand started to close around the doorknob when he drew it back. A faint glow of dim lamplight seeped out from beneath the door.

Fargo drew the big Colt, moved to the side, and used his left hand to noiselessly turn the knob. He felt the

111

latch open, flung the door in, and leaped into the room, the Colt ready to fire. His finger trembled on the trigger, loosened as he saw the china-blue eyes peering at him, dark with anger. Janet rose from the edge of the bed. "Where the hell have you been?" she demanded.

He closed the door, holstered the Colt, and faced her. "You shouldn't ever do that," he said. "It's one way to get yourself a bullet."

"Where have you been?" she repeated. He met her eyes, no irritation there, deep, raging fury. "I've been here for over an hour and now I have to get back."

"Didn't expect you'd be here tonight. You didn't say anything about it," he told her.

"Dean and Daddy went off to inspect some stock. I had a chance to get away," she said. "You haven't answered me, dammit. Where've you been?"

"Down at the dance hall," he said.

Her eyes grew wide with fury. "The dance hall? With some whore? You run off to some whore the first night you get here? I haven't been able to satisfy you?"

"Whoa, easy, now," he said, surprised at her fury. "I just had a few bourbons. No girl, just a few drinks."

She eyed him with suspicion. "No girl?" she pushed back.

"No girl," he said.

Her round face grew rounder, the fury beginning to fade, but her mouth going into a still-angry pout. "There'd better not be," she muttered.

"Damn, you've a temper," he said.

"The night's gone to waste," she accused. "I haven't more than fifteen minutes left now."

"That's a quarter of an hour," he said, pulling her to him. He flicked the buttons of her shirt open, closed his hand around one round breast.

"Aaah," she gasped, and he felt her body go soft. "Oh, damn." He pressed her back across the bed and showed

112

her how much could be done in fifteen minutes. It wasn't hard, not with the franticness that instantly erupted in her. She was still drawing in long breaths when she pulled clothes back on and went to the door to lean against him for a moment.

"Tomorrow night?" he asked. "I want to know this time."

"No. Daddy's giving a small dinner party. Dean will be away for the day and mightn't get back in time, so I have to play hostess," she said. Fargo's thoughts began to race at once. "The day after," she said. "I'll come into town in the afternoon. We'll have the whole day together."

"Good," he said, trying not to sound too distracted as Janet hurried off. He closed the door, felt the tightness of his jaw. Was Dean Thornbury off to drop instructions for new hired hands? Or to make his preparations alone? Fargo stretched out on the bed, sure of only one thing. He'd be at Amity's tomorrow night. He needed to get back to her anyway, to see how much time she had been able to get. He'd go under cover of darkness and he frowned as thoughts of Sam Tracy and his deputy swam into the forefront of his mind. He couldn't dismiss Sam Tracy, not yet. He grimaced as he turned the lamp off and let sleep throw itself around him.

6

He slept late, let the body renew itself, dressed, breakfasted, and strolled leisurely through town. He paused to
peer in at the dance hall. It was dark and empty except
for a boy sweeping the floor, and he moved on to the
stable, checked on the pinto's foreleg. Satisfied there was
no return of swollen tendons, he went on to walk to the
end of town. At the sheriff's office he saw Sam Tracy inside at a desk, waited, lounged against the edge of a
building across the street. The deputy, Ned, didn't appear and finally Fargo walked back through town. Did
Sam Tracy have the deputy watching Amity's place, he
wondered. Dammit, pieces with Sam Tracy's name on
them kept falling into place. Like a toothache, Sam
Tracy refused to go away.

Fargo returned to the hotel with still more time to use
up and decided to take apart the Colt and his big
Sharps rifle. He gave each a thorough and needed clean-
ing as dusk lowered itself over the town. When he finished, night blanketed Hillsville. He rode the pinto from
the stable, looked at the lights of the dance hall flickering on invitingly. He headed out of town, made a wide,
lazy circle that would bring him to Amity Sawyer's from
the rear. His eyes scanned the darkness, only a slender
moon hanging high. He rode slowly, pausing often as he
neared the house. The night was still, too still, night
birds made quiet, disturbed. He felt his skin growing

cold, the tiny hairs at the back of his neck rising. Something was wrong, his sixth sense at work. It had never failed him before. He dismounted, moved forward on foot, the pinto following his slow, measured steps. His eyes moved back and forth across the dark treetops, watching for a sign of movement while his ears strained to catch the slightest sound.

But he saw nothing and heard nothing as he came into sight of Amity's house, the lighted windows casting yellow funnels into the night. He halted, scanned the terrain once more, saw nothing, and moved forward, working his way around the far side of the house to leave the pinto sheltered in the shadows. He dropped beneath one funnel of light and made his way to the door, rapped softly. He heard the footsteps on the other side.

"Who is it?" Amity's voice called.

"Fargo," he answered softly.

She opened the door, the rifle in hand, stepped back to let him slip inside. Joseph Todd watched from beside the doorway to the dining room, a dish in one hand, and Jimmy came from the hallway, shirtless and with one sock off.

"Good evening, Mr. Fargo," Joseph said in his round, low voice. "It's good to see you again."

"Good to see you, Joseph," Fargo said as Amity put the rifle in a corner of the room. He glanced at Jimmy. "You look like you were on your way to bed," he said.

"Yes, sir," the boy answered.

"Good night," Fargo said, and followed with a smile to make the words less abrupt.

"On your way, Jimmy," Amity said, and Fargo watched as the boy shuffled his way down the dim long hallway to the very end where he disappeared into the last room, closed the door behind him. Fargo turned his eyes on Amity. The sound of Joseph washing dishes drifted in from the kitchen. He didn't need to put the question into words. "Day after tomorrow," she said.

"Too soon." He frowned.

She shrugged helplessly. "It's the best I could do. The arrangements are all made."

"Does Joseph know?" Fargo asked.

"He knows we'll be going," she said. "Nothing more."

"Too soon, dammit," Fargo muttered again.

"You said you'd ride with us," she reminded him.

"I was hoping I wouldn't need to," he said, and saw the questions form in the hazel eyes. "I planted a seed. It brought Dean Thornbury hightailing it back here. I wanted the time to see what else it would bring."

"You still think it's him," Amity said.

"Almost everything points to him," Fargo said.

"Almost?"

"Sam Tracy's in the picture yet," he told her, and saw the surprise in her eyes. "He's managed to be too near too often," Fargo said.

"You've cut out everybody else," she said.

"Pretty much."

"No hired killer from outside?"

"Can't see it. It's somebody who's lived a long spell in these parts, who knows the land like the back of his hand." He fell silent with his own thoughts. One fact burned into him. He had only two days to force the slave hunter into the open, only two days to trigger a move that would finally strip away a killer's mask. Not enough time, he repeated silently, not enough time for what he had set in motion to pay off. Perhaps there was no way but to ride out with Amity and Joseph, and he shook his head in angry frustration at the thought. That gave the slave hunter all the options, let the killer hold all the cards. Fargo's thoughts were still casting around for another answer when the night erupted, exploding from silence into a thunderous noise.

The first hail of bullets sent window glass flying into the room. "Down," he yelled as he dived. His arm reached out, clamped itself around Amity's legs, and brought her crashing down half atop him. Another volley of rifle fire slammed into the room, shattering the lamp, and he heard the pounding of hooves racing back and forth outside.

"Stay down," he called to Joseph in the kitchen as Amity clutched him in the darkness. The walls seemed to shake as volley after volley raked the house from end to end, the sharp crash of shattered glass mingling with the dull thud of bullets. He heard the scream, cutting through the other sounds. "No, let go of me . . . owoooo."

"Jimmy!" Amity shouted, tore out of his arms, and started to leap to her feet.

Fargo yanked her back as another hail of bullets swept into the room, smashing into the wall just over her head. He heard the horses galloping and the explosion of rifle fire ended as abruptly as it had begun. He let Amity tear from his grip this time and she ran down the hallway. He was on his feet as he heard her scream. A flicker of light cut into the darkness and Joseph appeared carrying a lamp.

"He's gone. They took Jimmy," Amity said, bursting into the room, her face made of horror and shock.

Fargo opened the door, the Colt in his hand, a matter of automatic habit. They were gone, he knew, and he felt Amity and Joseph behind him. His eyes swept the stillness, halted at the hitching post. A square of paper draped across one end, fastened by a single nail driven into the wood. He was at it in two long strides, tore it loose, and brought it back into the house, held it under the light of the small lamp. The words were printed in large, unruly letters:

"My God. Oh, my God," Fargo heard Amity breathe over his shoulder.

"Son of a bitch," Fargo swore softly. Joseph had stepped close enough to read the note and Fargo saw the shadowed pain come into the dark face. Amity stood as if transfixed, her arms rigid at her sides, her eyes round pools of shock. Fargo let the note fall onto the sofa and felt more than seething inside him, surprise that shouldn't have been there, an unwillingness to accept the full meaning of what had happened with such suddenness. He saw Amity's lips move, no sound from them, then the words finally following, hoarse, almost whispered.

"He's done it," she murmured.

Fargo felt Joseph's eyes on him, met the man's probing stare.

"The slave hunter?" Joseph said, not really a question, and Fargo nodded. "I expected as much. I knew Miss Amity was keeping something from me," he said calmly.

Amity continued to stare at Fargo and he watched her find hoarse words again. "Different, this time, but he's done it," she said, her voice trancelike.

"Yes, different," Fargo echoed, his eyes narrowed.

Amity raised her hands, turned, buried her face in them, and a half-muffled, agonized sound came from her. Fargo watched as Joseph went to her, gently pulled her hands from her face. "I'll saddle me a horse, Miss Amity," he said softly.

"No," Amity almost screamed, and Fargo saw her cheeks were stained with wetness. "No, Joseph, I can't let you do that."

Joseph's voice was calm, quietly reasoned. "He'll kill Jimmy. That man will kill Jimmy. You know it, Miss Amity," he said. Amity's pain-racked face mirrored the

118

terrible truth in his words, and she nodded, her head moving as if it were a puppet's. Joseph started to turn away from her. "I'll get me that horse," he said.

"*No!*" The word tore from her throat. "I can't let you do that, Joseph . . . I can't."

"You can't let him kill Jimmy," Joseph said quietly. Amity stared back in horror as, inside herself, she was torn in two. "It's got to be my way, Miss Amity," Joseph said. "I'm an old man. I've lived my life, a good one thanks to your daddy. Jimmy's got his whole young life ahead of him. We can't take that away from him."

Amity shook her head, her eyes half closed, giving herself up to the total helpless frustration and pain that racked her. Fargo's voice, cold as steel, cut into the air, his eyes going to Joseph first, then to Amity.

"No riding and no deciding," he bit out. "Not till I get back."

Joseph understood the hardness in the big man's eyes. "Won't he see you?" he asked. "Won't he be watching the house, waiting for me to ride out?"

"Soon, but not yet," Fargo said. "You two stay inside, in the dark." He was at the door in one long-legged stride, slipped outside, and raced around the side of the house to where he'd left the pinto. He was riding down the road seconds later, bent low in the saddle. The moon was a little fuller, its pale light a fraction brighter, but no tracking moon. It'd be slow and careful trailing. But the coin had another side. They wouldn't be going too far.

He followed the tracks on the road easily enough, saw them go on for a few hundred yards, halt where thick brush bordered both sides of the road. He quickly saw where they had turned to the right, trampling down a wide swath of brush by riding in a pack, bunched close together. Fargo followed their trail with ease and his eyes narrowed. Signs were like words, they often said a

119

great deal more than they seemed to say, he mused. The trail led over a ridge, up onto another that ended facing a narrow pathway atop the ridgeline and a thick stand of box elder. Fargo dismounted to kneel on the grass, letting his fingers feel along the pressed-down blades. He nodded to himself after a moment. They had shifted into single file and gone into the trees.

He swung onto the pinto and followed, moving slowly, pausing every few yards to dismount, press the grass, and make certain he still had the trail in the near-total blackness of the trees. He forced himself to stay with the agonizingly slow pace. A hasty mistake could cost him everything. Finally the stand of box elders came to an end. Their tracks bunched up almost instantly as they continued on riding in a close pack. There had to be five or six, at least, he guessed.

He followed the trail down a grassy slope, then parallel to a line of red cedars, and he suddenly reined the pinto to a halt, swerved the horse into the deepest shadows. In the distance a lone horseman raced across the top of a slope, heading back toward Amity Sawyer's house. The horse and rider were only a fast-moving silhouette that quickly vanished. Fargo, his lips tight, continued on, following the trail along the grassy slope. The open land turned into tree cover again and he weaved his way through the tree trunks until once again he reined up quickly.

His nostrils quivered, the faint sharp smell of wood smoke drifting through the still night air. He moved on carefully, slid from the horse, and proceeded on foot. The smell grew stronger and the land rose gently through the trees. He was on one knee as he reached the top of the rise, the cabin directly in front of him, set in a small hollow amid the trees that encircled it. He hid the pinto in the trees and moved closer, saw the smoke spiraling up from a short, stone chimney at one end of the log cabin. He counted five horses tethered outside and his brow furrowed. Once again, the signs held more than one meaning to him.

The cabin had a lone window that faced him and he left the tree cover to go forward in a crouching lope, silent as a lynx making for a henhouse. Wavering fireplace light flickered from the window as he crept up to it. His back pressed against the cabin, he straightened up alongside the window, darted a glance inside, and drew back at once. Five men, each holding a rifle, seated on the floor and leaning against three walls of the cabin. Jimmy, in only pajama bottoms, hands bound, had been put in the center of the room. Even in the quick glance, Fargo had seen the hollow-eyed fear in the boy's face. Fargo slid down into his crouch, moved soundlessly back to the nearby trees.

His lips became a hard line as he turned over his options. There were damn few. Rushing them would be suicide. They were too far apart to get more than three if he burst in on them. The others would cut him in two with rifle fire. A shot through the window might make them come out firing, give him a chance to at least even the odds. But he discarded the thought as quickly as it had come to him. It might also make them hole up inside, with Jimmy still their hostage. No good, he muttered to himself. He had to make them come out on their own, not expecting trouble. The few precious seconds of surprise would spell the difference between winning and losing. He rested on one knee as he stared at the cabin. It was beginning to resemble a small fortress as the minutes ticked inexorably away, stretched into hours.

The spiral of smoke grew heavier as inside new logs were placed on the fire and Fargo watched the gray cloud drift upward. Suddenly he sat up straight, his lips moving into a tight smile. He was on his feet at once, hurrying to the pinto; he slung the big Sharps rifle over his shoulder and took a blanket from his saddlebag.

Moments later he was circling the cabin in his long, loping stride, bringing up at the rear of it where a thick-trunked box elder hung a long branch almost to the edge of the cabin roof. He began to climb the tree, slide his way along the branch until, as he neared the end, it began to dip. He half-turned, clutching the branch with both hands, swung himself back and forth, each swing bringing him nearer the edge of the roof. Stretching his long legs, he caught one foot atop the wood of the roof as he swung again, held himself there, pulled his hands along the branch as far as he dared. The crack of a branch would end everything. Getting a hold with the toe of his other foot, he pushed himself free, dropped to his hands and knees at the very edge of the roof.

He stayed motionless, drawing in his breath, then rose on tiptoe. Moving one step at a time, the blanket under his arm, he made his way on catlike steps until he reached the stone of the chimney. He halted, opened the blanket fully, and draped it over the opening of the chimney. He watched the center of the blanket puff up as the smoke pushed against it. The smoke would gather, first at the top, until it filled the chimney space, then plunge downward in a whooshing back rush to hurl from the fireplace in a suffocating, choking cloud. He watched the center of the blanket push upward for another few moments as the pressing smoke roiled beneath its cover, still seeking a way out. Lowering himself to his haunches, he slid across the slope of the roof to the other side. Bringing the big Sharps around, he put it to his shoulder, his finger poised on the trigger.

He had but a few seconds more to wait when he heard the shouts from inside the cabin. The door flew open, the figures stumbling out half-cloaked in a smoky haze, two first, then a third, the last two following, Jimmy stumbling out by himself.

"Goddamn," one man cursed. "Goddamn chimney's backed up." The kidnappers coughed and hacked, cursed as they waved at the cloud of smoke that followed them outside. Fargo drew a bead on the nearest two who had started to look up toward the roof. The big Sharps rifle fired twice and an explosion of red spattered into the gray of the smoke.

"Shit!" he heard another voice shout, followed the third figure in line as the man started to race for the trees. He fired through the drifting smoke, saw the figure seem to half-somersault forward, strike the ground, and twist again, fall sideways, arms and legs flung out like a broken doll.

"He's on the roof," one of the last two called, and a volley of shots instantly slammed into the slope of the wood, two pinging into the stone of the chimney just behind him. The two men had flung themselves in opposite directions, reached the deep shadows at the edge of the trees, and Fargo ducked flat as another hail of bullets slammed into the roof inches from where he crouched. The smoke had almost cleared away, the fire blown out by the back rush, and they were able to focus on him now. He scrambled up the sloping roof, flipped across the peak to the other side as four shots splintered bits of wood close enough to send slivers into his cheek. As he slid down the other side, he wiped them off, felt the trickle of blood against his face. He landed on the ground with both feet, legs crouched to absorb the impact, raced to one corner of the cabin.

"Drop your guns," he called out. The answer was another cluster of shots that thudded into the wood of the cabin, most a little high this time.

"He's behind the cabin," he heard the nearest man

call, his voice gravelly. "You watch that side, I'll take this one," the man ordered. "Keep him boxed in back there."

Fargo drew backward, moving in a crouch on silent feet. He slipped into the trees and began to make his way around the edge of the treeline, turning and twisting his body so not a branch was disturbed. His eyes flicked at the cabin as he moved ghostlike through the trees, saw Jimmy on the ground, huddled against the wall near the open door. Fargo, crouched, ducked low under a cluster of branches, peered ahead, followed the crisscross lines of the low branches, halted as he picked out the black silhouette of the man's crouching shape. He raised the Sharps to his shoulder, took aim.

"Don't move and drop the gun," he said, his voice just loud enough for the man to hear. He saw the shape spin, saw the flash of the gunpowder as the first shot whistled through the branches, fired too hurriedly and way off to the right. The gunman never got his second shot off as Fargo fired. The heavy rifle slug tore into the dark shape and Fargo saw the man half-rise, turn, stumble out of the trees into the little clearing. The figure staggered, turned toward him, and where there should have been a chest there was a caved-in hole that was rapidly turning a dark red. Fargo watched as the man fell backward with a final shuddered groan, lay still on the ground.

Fargo peered at the other side of the half-circle of trees, the last gunman too well hidden to see at that distance. "Come out, your hands in the air," Fargo called. "I won't say it twice."

"Not me, you bushwhackin' bastard. You, you're coming out," he heard the man answer. "I got my gun aimed right at that kid's head. You come out or I'll blow his damn head off."

Fargo felt the wave of surprise and helpless rage

sweep over him. The man had struck back with the cunning of a cornered rat. Fargo swore in bitter fury, aware that he was the trapped one now. The man held the trump card, Jimmy's life.

"Throw the rifle out first," the man called, sensing Fargo's silence for what it was, helplessness.

Fargo muttered an oath as he flung the rifle into the open. "The gun belt," the man called, and Fargo obeyed, tossed it out where it landed almost atop the rifle. He stepped forward, out of the trees, his eyes on the nearby branches, watching as the man came out, a heavy Whitneyville Walker Colt in his hand. He was of medium height, black-haired, with a face that glared out from under low, beetling brows.

"I just wanted a look at you before I blow you apart," the man growled. "Son of a bitch, you did a lot of damage."

"Not enough," Fargo grunted.

The man stepped closer and Fargo eyed the heavy Walker. His muscles twitched as he held back the impulse to rush the man. He'd only get a slug ripping into his belly, he realized, the gun held unwaveringly. He saw the man's finger start to tighten on the trigger.

"This is the end of the line for you, mister," the man muttered. The quick, scraping sound interrupted and Fargo's eyes flicked to the cabin to see Jimmy leaping to his feet, starting to run, racing to disappear around the corner of the cabin. The man's head spun toward the boy for an instant. The split second was all the Trailsman needed. With the lightning-fast reactions of a cougar, he sprang, slamming into the man, one big hand closing around the butt of the gun.

Dimly aware that Jimmy had vanished around the corner of the cabin, Fargo went down clinging to the man, pressing his gun hand backward. "Bastard," he heard the man hiss, felt a fist sink into his ribs, ignored the blow, twisted the hand further until the gun dropped from pain-racked fingers. The man got a leg up, pushed his knee into Fargo's belly, and the Trailsman rolled away. The man half-turned, tried to reach the gun, but Fargo brought a sledgehammer blow onto the back of his reaching fingers.

"Owoooo, Christ," the man cried out in pain. Fargo, on one knee, lifted a looping left that caught the man on the side of his face, sending him sprawling across the ground.

Fargo rose to his feet, took a step forward, and grabbed the man by the shirt front, started to yank him up. A double-handed blow took him by surprise, dug into his abdomen, and he fell back as breath rushed out of him. The kidnapper rushed at him, swinging a round-house left. Fargo managed to duck away so the blow only grazed his cheekbone. But, off balance, he fell sideways, landed on his hands and knees, looked up to see the man diving for his Walker. Fargo measured distance in the blink of an eye. The man's hand was just touching the butt of the Colt. Fargo saw his own gun belt a half-dozen feet closer. He rolled, came up on one knee at the gun belt just as the man brought his Walker up. Diving sideways, Fargo yanked his own Colt from the holster as two shots tore across the back of his shirt. He fired, dived, fired again. The man got off another shot, but Fargo heard the sound of it going into the trees as he rolled, came up to fire again, held back as the man's figure seemed to sway in a tight circle. Fargo, ready to blast another shot into the swaying figure, saw the man slowly sink down onto both knees, almost as if in prayer. Perhaps he was taking a last such moment, Fargo reflected idly, watched the figure pitch forward onto its face to shudder once and lay still.

Fargo rose, gun still trained on the man, walked to the silent form, and pushed with the tip of his foot, felt the lifelessness in the figure. He stepped back, scooped up his own gun belt, and strapped it on as he called out to Jimmy. The boy's head poked around the corner of the cabin, his face pale and shaken even in the dim moonlight. Jimmy took another tentative step forward, then burst out to race to where the big man waited. "Give me your hands," Fargo said, untied the wrist bonds as Jimmy stretched his arms out.

"Amity? Joseph?" Jimmy asked, his voice full of fear.

"They're all right," Fargo said. "There's a tree close behind the cabin. It'll get you on the roof. Get my blanket down from the chimney while I clean up around here."

As Jimmy scurried off, Fargo dragged the last of the kidnappers into the trees where he'd stashed away the others. He had just returned to the little half-circle when Jimmy appeared with the blanket, handed it to him neatly rolled. "Now go inside and get a fire started again," Fargo said. "I want the place looking just the way he left it when he rides in."

Fargo carried the blanket to where he'd hidden the pinto, and when he returned, a small spiral of smoke was once more coming from the chimney. Fargo took Jimmy outside with him as he closed the cabin door, stepped back into the treeline. He looked back, surveyed the scene, the cabin door shut, the smoke drifting out of the chimney, firelight flickering through the window. Satisfied there was nothing to tell that there was anything wrong, Fargo moved farther back into the trees with Jimmy. He sat down, the big Sharps on the ground beside him. Jimmy lowered himself to the ground beside the big man.

"When he comes back, no matter what happens, you stay in here," Fargo said. "Understand?"

Jimmy nodded gravely. "How long do we have?" Jimmy asked.

"It'll be dawn soon enough," Fargo said. "You just settle down. It's time you started learning how to wait."

Jimmy fell silent and Fargo let the boy stir his own thoughts as he fixed his eyes on the tops of the trees at the other edge of the semicircle. Time seemed to hang motionless, but the moon had dropped from view and Fargo knew that the dawn waited impatiently. When the first pale tint touched the top edge of the trees to suddenly outline the uppermost leaves, Fargo rose on one knee. A little while later he shifted to a crouch, picked up the rifle. As the gray became dawn, his eyes moved to the opposite bank of trees and he stood up half behind a thick elderberry trunk.

He heard the horse before he saw it, moving fast through the trees, no attempt at stealth. The dark figure came into view, winding through the thick tree cover. In what seemed an hour but was only minutes, the figure rode into the little clearing in front of the cabin. Fargo stared, felt the frown digging into his forehead, a slow, silent oath forming on his lips. Surprise, shock, an astonishment that approached disbelief flooded over him as he continued to stare at the horseman, at the dotted red kerchief, and above it, Henson's overbearing, bully face. The frown dug deeper into him as he watched Henson swing from the horse.

"Inside, there," Henson shouted, anger in his voice. "Bring the goddamn kid out." Fargo saw Henson peer at the cabin, wait, then the frown start to gather on his face at the silence. "You hear me in there, dammit?" Henson shouted.

Fargo stepped noiselessly from the trees, the rifle ready to fire in his hands. "They won't hear anything anymore," he said softly.

128

Henson whirled, his hand going for his gun, freezing in midair as he saw the barrel of the big Sharps leveled at his chest.

"That's being smart," Fargo said, saw Henson bring his eyes up from the rifle to stare at the big man in front of him. "Take your gun out, two fingers, nice and slow," Fargo ordered. Henson's eyes became tiny fragments of pure hate as he lifted his gun from the holster, tossed it on the ground. Fargo took a step closer to the man, kicked the gun aside.

"You been waiting for me to come back," Henson growled.

"That's right," Fargo said. "Dean Thornbury tell you Amity planned to take off on her own with Joseph?" he asked.

"Go to hell," Henson snarled.

Using the rifle barrel as a lance, Fargo rammed the end into Henson's stomach.

"Owooo, Christ," the man gasped as he doubled over and fell to his knees, both hands clutching his midsection.

"Who told you? How'd you hear?" Fargo asked.

On his knees, Henson shook his head. "Screw you," he muttered.

Fargo brought the butt of the rifle down against the man's forehead, a scraping blow.

Henson pitched forward, his temple a red, raw expanse of scraped flesh. "Oh, Christ," he muttered into the ground. Slowly, he drew himself back onto his knees, saw Fargo lift the rifle butt again.

"Thornbury tell you?" Fargo asked again.

Henson shook his head, pressed a sleeve against his raw, bleeding temple. "Heard him talking about it," he muttered.

"To who?" Fargo barked.

"His pa, just his pa," Henson said.

"So you figured to move fast," Fargo said.

Henson's eyes held hate through their fear and pain as he looked up at the big man. "I told you she wouldn't get away with it. Nobody makes a fool out of me," he said.

"That makes you wrong again," Fargo bit out. "Get up." He lowered the barrel of the rifle for a moment, misjudging the man's desperation. Henson started to get up, hurled himself into a lurching dive to grab hold of the end of the rifle barrel with both hands, forcing it down, and Fargo's shot buried itself into the ground. Fargo kicked out, slammed his foot into the man's side. But Henson's grip on the gun barrel was a vise of fear, hate, and desperation. It stayed as he fell sideways, his falling weight tearing the gun from Fargo's hands.

Henson, still clutching the barrel, landed on his side, opened his fingers to bring the rifle around, but Fargo was at him instantly, looping a long, flat swing of his left fist that struck the stock of the rifle just forward of the comb. The blow sent the gun flying from Henson's hands as he tried to turn it. He started to dive after it, but Fargo's knee came down onto his belly and he cried out in pain, rolled away.

Fargo tried to bring a blow downward into the man's face, but Henson managed to twist his head to the side, got a leg raised, and Fargo felt himself being half-lifted, half-turned aside. He landed on his hands and knees, leaped to his feet to see Henson barreling into him. He managed to bring up a short stiff uppercut, felt it slam into the man's jaw, but Henson shook it off, wrapped both arms around him, and tried to wrestle him to the ground. Fargo braced himself, using the powerful muscles of his long legs, spun Henson in a half-circle, and flung him away as though he were a doll.

He went after the man as Henson started to get to his feet, caught him with a blow alongside the head that would ordinarily have brought him down. But Henson was fired with the extra strength of a wild and desperate man and he shook off the blow, came back swinging wildly. Fargo avoided the blows, took them on his arms, stepped back, and brought a thunderous blow downward over Henson's arms. It smashed into the man's face and he went down, started to get up, shaking his head. Fargo whistled a looping left that caught him alongside the other side of his face and Henson fell backward, half-rolled, sprawled across the ground. Fargo moved toward him again and Henson pulled himself to his knees, suddenly hurled himself sideways, and Fargo saw the big Sharps on the ground only a foot from the man. He dived forward as Henson closed his hands around the rifle, started to swing the barrel around. Fargo kicked out, his foot hitting the rifle just under the trigger guard as Henson brought the gun up.

The shot exploded as the rifle barrel flew upward and Fargo saw Henson's face disappear, blow away in a cascading shower of flesh, bone, and blood. He ducked away from the fragments that filled the air, and when he looked back, Henson was a faceless form on the ground, a sickening, stomach-turning apparition. Fargo felt his lips draw back in disgust as he scooped up the rifle and turned away.

Jimmy, against a tree, kept his face averted and Fargo let a deep breath of air come up from the bottom of his chest. He reached the boy, took his arm, and steered him into the trees to where he had left the pinto.

He rode back slowly, Jimmy sitting behind him, his thoughts churning, his face harsh, a frown still lining his brow. As he reached Amity's house, the two figures raced out, Amity first, Joseph close behind her. Jimmy slid down over the pinto's rump and was swept up in welcoming embraces as Fargo dismounted, waited silently. Finally, wiping her eyes, Amity turned to him.

"We owe you again," she said. "Much more than there's any way to pay back." He watched the hazel eyes search his face, the question stark inside them.

"Henson," he said quietly.

Surprise widened her eyes at once. "Henson," she echoed. "So you were wrong all along."

He didn't answer and watched her turn to Joseph, relief flooding her face. "It's over, Joseph. Did you hear? We can make it now."

Fargo heard the word drop from his lips, a dull, terrible sound. "No," he said, and Amity turned to him, stared. "It's not over," he said.

"What are you talking about?" she asked.

"Henson wasn't the slave hunter," Fargo said quietly.

She stared at him and he saw the refusal to believe gather in her eyes. "Of course he was. You saw him with your own eyes. You just said it was Henson," she flared.

"I know what I said," he returned. "I said Henson was behind this."

"Then he had to be the slave hunter. You told me yourself you expected the slave hunter to strike. Now that it's happened you're saying it didn't happen? That doesn't make any sense. It all fits, points to Henson," she countered.

"It only fits on the surface," Fargo said with quiet certainty.

"That's ridiculous. Maybe you just can't accept being wrong all along," she flung back.

"Henson wasn't the slave hunter," Fargo said.

He saw the fear in her eyes, the rejection of words that tore aside hope and relief. "Dammit, how can you say that?" she almost shouted.

"The slave hunter works alone. He may hire hands, but he works alone. And he plans every step, with care. He covers his tracks, makes every move carefully. He'd never have let the whole pack of them ride off together with Jimmy. They were too easy to follow. He'd have had them scatter and he'd have taken the boy alone. If he had to have them hold Jimmy, he'd have posted guards. It was a wild, sloppy operation. It didn't carry his mark, none of it. Henson wasn't the slave hunter," he said again.

"You're making a lot out of little things. That's no proof, none of it. Maybe you're reading it all wrong. Maybe he had to change his usual way of doing things this time. Ever think of that?" she tossed back.

Fargo turned away, unwilling to gun down hope any further, and swung onto the pinto.

"You're an obstinate, unyielding man," Amity shouted at him.

"That's right," he said as he turned the pinto, prodded the horse into a walk.

"Where are you going?" she asked.

"To see about being obstinate," he said.

"Will you still ride with us tomorrow?" she called after him.

"You can be damn sure of it, one way or the other," he said as he pushed the pinto into a trot. He slowed only after he turned the corner of the road and headed the horse toward Hillsville. Amity's question clung as he rode. Had the slave hunter changed his ways? Had he needed to give up his usual careful planning, his trust in loneness? Fargo shook his head in rejection. The question only seemed logical. A fox can't change the way it hunts. It can't throw off cunning and caution. Those things are part of the creature. The way of a hawk on the hunt is its own. Henson was not the slave hunter,

Fargo murmured to himself, not without bitterness. The final answer still hid in the pieces that refused to come together. And time was nearly gone. He spurred the pinto on faster.

7

Fargo reached the hotel room before the town came fully awake, undressed, and fell onto the bed. It had been twenty-four hours since he'd last slept and he fell into a heavy sleep at once. It was past the noon hour when he woke, went down to the bathroom at the end of the hall, and doused himself under the pail that served as a shower, the cold water washing away the last clinging hold of sleep. He returned to his room, only a towel wrapped around his lithe-muscled body, lay down across the bed, and let the towel continue to absorb the water still on his skin. His thoughts turned to the unanswered question that still stayed hidden away. Not just a question, no abstract exercise, but the key to life or death, happiness or sorrow.

His lips drew tight in irritation as his mind raced. The seed he'd planted had brought results, but unexpected ones. Yet it was still there. It could still bring that final answer he had expected. But the picture had changed, time turning it all upside down. He couldn't wait any longer, hope for the seed to take further root. He had to try and prepare for the strike that was certain to come, and he felt his face twisting in disgust. It was a little like fighting with a blindfold on. You could only guess where the blow would come from. But guessing was all he had left and he closed his eyes, began to draw upon the mental maps that were filed away inside his head.

Amity had said they'd take Boulder Road, he pondered. That meant they'd go northeast through the low line of boulders that gave the road its name. He frowned as he focused on the terrain in his mind. The low boulders lined both sides for at least two miles and then the left side of the road stayed level, bordered by shag brush, the right side rising in a low slope. Fargo went over each yard in his mind as though he were walking it off on the pinto. Another mile or so along the road it curved, ran through a sudden and steep collection of high rock formations that rose on both sides and spread out for miles. The area had been given the name of Staghorn Hills and Fargo opened his eyes, peered into space with his jaw setting grimly. Staghorn Hills was the best place, the logical place to strike. It afforded a perfect view of the road and a dozen ideal spots to wait, to line up the single, killing bull's-eye shot that was the mark of the slave hunter. And just as important, Staghorn Hills offered the perfect place to get away, the high rock formations a honeycomb of passages.

Staghorn Hills, Fargo grunted to himself, but his eyes narrowed for another moment. There was one more spot, where the road curved and Staghorn Hills began to form. It had none of the perfect advantages of Staghorn Hills, but it was a possibility. It couldn't be ignored, Fargo mused, and he'd have to be ready to make his move before the wagon reached it. From there, he'd have to be prepared for Staghorn Hills, especially where the high stones closed to form a rough arch over the road.

Fargo put his hands behind his head, continued to make plans, and he was still lying across the bed with only the towel around him when Janet arrived. He let her in at her soft knock, took in the pale-lime shirt and the matching skirt that made her look light and airy as a slice of chiffon pie. In the china-blue eyes, instant, darkening stirrings glinted as she took in his towel-clad form. Her hands moved across his chest. "You're being unfair. I've shopping to do first. I drove in with the buckboard," she said, half-pouting.

"You'll get done with it faster now." He grinned back as he reached for his shirt.

"Indeed," she said, devoured him with her eyes as he dressed. She gave him a sidelong glance as he picked up his gun belt. "I've something to ask you," she said, her tone careful.

"Ask," he said, strapping on the gun belt.

She drew a deep breath. "Henson didn't return to the bunkhouse last night. My father sent some men out looking for him. He was last seen riding out of town with five men. He was found this morning, the others, too." She let her lips purse thoughtfully. "Would you know anything about that?" she asked.

"Maybe," he said carefully.

"I suspected as much," Janet said. "What stupid thing did he try this time?"

"It's done with," Fargo said curtly. "You've shopping to do."

He opened the door for her and she left with him, knowing he'd not say more. "Maybe you'll feel more talkative sometime," she commented.

"I doubt it," he said as he went out into the afternoon sunlight with her, followed her to the feed store, helped her to get four sacks of feed to the buckboard.

"Ollie's General Store next," Janet said, taking his arm as they walked down the street. They were opposite the dance hall when she saw a newly carved wooden rocker outside a carpenter's shop. "Wait a moment," she said as she strode to the chair, began to examine it.

Fargo leaned against a hitching rail as the girl emerged from the Royal Palace, red hair a brassy cap atop her wide, flat face, her big-boned body swinging, the heavy breasts half out of the tight silk dress. Her eyes lighted at once as she spotted him.

"Well, hello there. I've been looking for you to come back," she said, sauntering up to him.

"Hello, Crystal," Fargo said. "Got anything for me?"

She hooked an arm into his, let one finger toy with the buttons of his shirt. "Anything you want, I've got, big boy," she murmured.

"You know what I mean," Fargo said.

"Not yet, but I keep listening," she answered, her finger still toying with his shirt. "Why don't you come with me now? I've got all afternoon for you," she cooed.

The voice cut through the air like a scythe. "Get away from him." Fargo saw Janet moving toward him from the shop, the china-blue eyes as cold as ice.

The dance-hall girl turned a disdainful stare at her. "You talking to me, honey?" she said, her voice taking on the hardness of the streets.

"Don't you call me honey and get your hands off him," Janet hissed.

"Fuck off," Crystal snapped. "I'm taking him with me."

"Whore!" Janet barked. "He's with me."

Crystal's voice became a harsh sneer. "Hell, you ain't woman enough for half of him," she said. "And watch your fucking tongue."

"Slut! Garbage!" Janet speared.

Fargo saw the dance-hall girl turn to face the small, compact form striding toward her.

"I'll bust your high-toned ass for you," the girl rasped.

Fargo moved to step in between them. "Janet, forget it," he said placatingly. Janet brushed past him and in her eyes he saw the pinpoints of fury. "Janet," he called.

"Stay out of this," she snapped. He reached for her arm, but she pulled it away from him and he saw her hand come around to smash across Crystal's face. "Stinking, filthy whore," she hissed. "I'll teach you to put your hands on him."

The dance-hall girl staggered back, as much in surprise as in pain, and Fargo saw Janet swing again. But this time Crystal blocked the blow, came around with a roundhouse swing that landed high atop Janet's blond hair. It carried enough power to make her compact form halt, the yellow hair bouncing in the air. Crystal started for her again, her face now twisted in anger, hands outstretched. He saw Janet duck under the girl's clutching hands and, a cotton-candy cannonball, her body barreled into the other girl, head lowered. Crystal doubled over, breath rushing from her, and Janet put an elbow into her throat and the dance-hall girl fell backward, one hand clutching Janet's arm, pulling her down with her.

"Damn," Fargo swore, but held back in a kind of surprised fascination. A crowd had rushed up at once, grew into a small mob in seconds, shouting, cheering, laughing. A half-dozen men jostled in front of him, but he could easily see over their heads. Janet and Crystal were rolling on the ground, Crystal a head taller and heavier, having a hard time holding off the small, compact raging fury. Both were gasping oaths and he saw Janet's hand in a ripping swipe tear down along the front of the tight silk dress and Crystal's breasts cascaded out to a roar from the crowd.

The bigger girl managed to get a leg up, shove it into Janet's side, and send her rolling away. Getting to her feet, she came at the smaller girl with both hands clawing. Again Janet ducked under, came up to rake the bigger girl's face with her own nails. Crystal stepped back, her face streaked with red marks. Fargo caught a glimpse of Janet's eyes as she half-spun, and he stared at the wild, raging fury he saw there. Janet flew at Crystal again to the shouts of the crowd, but this time the bigger girl used her size and weight, turned sideways, catching Janet with a hip blow. Fargo saw the lime-green blouse, hanging in shreds, stagger to a halt from the blow. Crystal swung her elbow, backhanded, catching Janet on the cheek.

"Damn," Fargo swore as he started to push his way through the whooping wall of onlookers that had formed in front of him. He saw Crystal grab for a fistful of Janet's blond hair but only catch a few strands as Janet swung the short locks. Crystal sank her teeth into Janet's shoulder and Fargo saw the smaller girl shudder in pain, but in her eyes the ice-cold fury only grew more stark. As he watched, tried to get to her, he saw Janet drive her fist into Crystal's eye. The dance-hall girl let go with a cry of pain, fell back against the edge of a watering trough. Janet shot forward and Fargo saw her eyes, insensate hate blazing in the ice-blue orbs. She smashed into the bigger girl, bent her backward into the water trough. Crystal struggled, but she was no match for the wild strength that came from the raging hate. She fell backward, into the trough, Janet's hands around her throat.

Reaching the front of the shoving crowd, Fargo saw Janet pushing Crystal's head into the trough, pull her out for a moment, then push her under again, her fingers steel claws around Crystal's throat. He heard her hoarse hiss of pure hate as she held the struggling figure under the water of the trough. "Bitch," she muttered. "Bitch, bitch, bitch. Nobody takes anything that's mine. Nobody takes anything from me, do you hear, slut? *Nobody!*"

Crystal was sending up bubbles of water, her struggles growing weak, her legs hanging over the side of the trough almost still.

"Damn, I think she's going to drown that girl," Fargo heard one of the onlookers say in awe.

"I believe she is, Lem," his companion agreed.

Fargo bulled his way forward, reached around Janet from behind, and grasped her arms. He tried to pull her hands free, but she refused to let go. "Damn," he swore as he yanked harder, tore her grip from the other girl's throat. He dragged her from the trough as others reached in to pull Crystal up. Janet struggled in his grip, swore, turned her head, and tried to bite him. He shook her hard and saw the blank hate in her eyes start to shatter. He cast a glance at the trough. Crystal was on the ground, two men holding her bent over as she heaved up great gasps of water. He brought his eyes back to Janet. The insensate fury was gone from her eyes and there was recognition there as she stared back at him, but the raging hate still lurked inside her.

Fargo stared back at her, his brow furrowed, and he kept hold of her arms as he watched the overwhelming fury slowly recede in her eyes. He was still staring at her when she spoke. "You can let go now," she said. He relaxed his hold and she met his probing, still-astonished stare, rubbed her arms where he'd gripped her. "Thanks for stopping me," she said. "I've a terrible temper."

"That's not the word for it," Fargo commented.

"I'd like to clean up," she said.

He nodded, turned to start back to the hotel. Janet took his arm and walked close beside him. He glanced back. Crystal was on her feet, a few bystanders still holding on to her as she swayed in the torn dress, her big body more naked than clothed. She still gasped in deep breaths, but she'd recover, he saw, looked at Janet beside him. She managed to somehow seem regally triumphant despite the shredded blouse, the scratched and dirt-smeared face, her chin carried high, almost haughty. At the room, he fetched a washcloth and a basin of water, helped clean off caked dirt, scratches, and applied some salve to the bite marks on her shoulder. She lay back on the bed when he finished, the shredded blouse

141

on the floor, the high, round breasts pointing upward, and he saw the dark pinpoints inside her eyes, the seething still there. As he watched, she slid the skirt from her, pushed herself up on both elbows, and opened her lips. "Come to me, Fargo," he heard her murmur. "Now come to me."

He sank down over her and she pushed her breasts into his face, his mouth, encircled his waist with both arms, pushing trousers from him. Her skin was on fire, a soft fire that sent a shiver of pleasure through him and he could feel the glowing of her as she swung over onto him, sank down on him, and half-screamed in pleasure. She pumped up and down over him, made love to him, thrashed and screamed and flung herself at him with a wildness beyond her usual turbulent desire. It was as if all the raging fury of the battle were still inside her and needed the inner release only his body could bring. Whatever the roots of it, she was awesomely magnificent, overwhelming in her wanting, and when dusk darkened the room and she lay beside him, he was as spent and satisfied as she.

He lay silently, moving over half atop her to study her round face, the china-blue eyes that had mirrored such wild, demonic rage but a few hours earlier. She saw the frown touch his forehead and her smile held a hint of smugness. "Still surprised?" she murmured.

"I guess so," Fargo said slowly.

"You shouldn't be," she said. "Not after all the times you've made love to me."

"I suppose not," he conceded, lay back, thought about her words. And about roots. She turned, pressed herself against his chest.

"I have to be going," she murmured. "And I want to stay."

"I won't be here tomorrow night," he said.

She rose up, speared him with a suddenly sharp

glance. "Why not?" she questioned. "Going to look in on Amity Sawyer?"

"Got some personal business to tend to," he said side-stepping the question.

Her eyes stayed on him for a moment, a half-pout sliding over her round face, and then she lay back. "Just as well, I suppose. I have to go over the month's receipts with Daddy tomorrow night. Dean's going to be gone for the day."

Fargo kept his voice even. "He's gone off to rustle up some contacts?" he remarked.

"Yes, as a matter of fact. He's gone to Boulder Hollow," Janet answered.

Fargo kept his glance mild as he studied her round face. Boulder Hollow lay some ten miles beyond the Staghorn Hills area, a small settlement fed by Boulder Road. The wagon would slow down there.

Fargo lay back on the bed, watched Janet as she began to dress. He waited till she was nearly finished when he swung to his feet, pulled on trousers, and turned to her. His eyes probed into her as he let the question fall casually from his lips.

"What would you say if I told you that Dean is the slave hunter?" he asked.

The frown appeared on her smooth forehead at once and she peered at him. "No, that's what I'd say. No, never," she answered. "You're all wrong."

"Things keep adding up," he said, his eyes watching her intently. He saw the rejection come into her face.

"No, I don't believe it. I don't care what seems to add up. I won't listen to any more of this," she flared.

He allowed a small tight smile, watched her as she drew the shredded blouse around herself, her round face almost pouting. She was silent as he walked to the buckboard with her, halted there to turn, reached her hand to his cheek. "You said you weren't going to concern yourself with it any longer, with Joseph Todd, Amity Sawyer, the slave hunter, all of it," she reminded him.

"You afraid I might be right?" he asked.

"No, I just don't want you hurt," she answered.

He smiled at the reply and knew there was no arguing with it.

"I will, soon enough," he told her.

She kissed him, a soft, tender kiss, and his eyes followed her as she climbed into the buckboard. He watched her drive away, stayed peering after her until the buckboard faded out of sight in the dark. His jaw was a hard, tight line as he walked back to the room. He lay down across the bed, turned time backward as he began going over each piece once again. When he finally closed his eyes to sleep, he lay wrapped in a grim blanket.

He slept late and woke with the bitter taste in his mouth, washed, and dressed, and the bitter taste stayed with him. The final answers waited, the truth that would be beyond changing. There was no turning away. He'd come too far for that. He saw the china-blue eyes in front of him when he'd told her about Dean, remembered how so many things churned in the depths of those blue orbs. He turned to the door as he strapped on his gun belt, took his gear, and hurried to the stable. Minutes later he rode out of town and he rode with a grim hope against hope that he was wrong, and he was surprised at how hard the feeling gripped him.

He took the road past Amity's house, reined up when he reached it. The front yard was empty, the barn closed. It seemed deserted until Amity appeared at the door, her tall, angular figure clothed in a brown dress that seemed improperly formal. "You're early," she commented.

"Yes," he agreed. "Where's the wagon?"

"In the barn," she answered.

"The others here yet?"

She nodded. "They're inside with Joseph."

"Jimmy?" Fargo questioned.

"Gone to stay with Mabel Hasslet," Amity said, her voice staying flat. "You coming in?"

"No, I'm riding ahead," he told her.

The hazel eyes studied him. "Still think the slave hunter is out there someplace?" she pushed at him.

"I'm an obstinate man, remember?" he answered, saw her face tighten. "I'll hook up with you later," he said, and felt her eyes watching as he rode away. He headed the pinto onto Boulder Road, set an easy but ground-eating pace. When he reached the slow curve just before Staghorn Hills, his eyes swept the terrain on both sides, his mouth turning in tightly. He rode on, espied the tall rock spires of the Staghorn Hills, rode on along the road, his eyes moving from side to side, watching, estimating, absorbing, seeing what most men would miss. He rode on, past the stone arch over the road, and continued, kept the pinto moving forward. Ten miles on lay Boulder Hollow and he rode steadily until he was out of the Staghorn Hills area, then suddenly he swerved the horse to the left, bounded up a narrow, steep pathway all the way to the top. He halted for a moment, turned the pinto, and rode back along the high land toward the Staghorn Hills, moving into the area from the back edge.

Carefully he maneuvered through the labyrinth of passages, making his way through one after the other in the honeycomb of defiles and crannies that formed the high rock formation. All the while, he climbed steadily toward the high places that let him look down on Boulder Road below. When he neared the very top, he swung down from the pinto, left the horse tucked away in a narrow, one-ended defile, and moved forward on foot. He reached the top of the rocks, found a high mound of stone that gave him a view of Boulder Road and of the surrounding rock formations. He sank back into a crevice and became a silent, motionless shape, tuning his cat's hearing to listen for every tiny sound. There were precious few, he found, the high rocks a silent place with not even a shrub to rustle from the wind that curled around the stones.

He waited, his lake-blue eyes turned frozen blue crystals, and the sound, when it first touched his ears, was exactly as he had expected, a confirmation, a lone horse's hooves, moving slowly, carefully. The sound grew closer, quietly sharp on the hard rock, and Fargo rose to his feet, peered out from the crevice. The sound of the horse suddenly ended and a tight, knowing smile touched the Trailsman's lean handsomeness. The rider was on foot now, and there was no further sound, the figure moving noiselessly across the rocks. Fargo's eyes were narrowed as they swept the surrounding area and he glimpsed the high-crowned black hat first, moving past a rounded boulder. He watched the path of the tip of the hat and then the figure came into view, the black outfit and black mask a stark contrast against the sun-baked rocks.

The figure halted atop a small flat rock wedged between two tall boulders. The spot commanded a perfect view of Boulder Road below and Fargo watched the figure sink to one knee, the rifle nestled in the crook of one arm. Fargo took another silent step from the crevice and he felt the bitterness welling up inside him. He had figured it right, the final answer in front of him, and he was less than happy for it as he thought of china-blue eyes that had pleaded with him to back off.

He crept forward, the big Colt heavy in his hand, circled a half-dozen stones to come up behind the crouching figure holding the rifle. He positioned himself against one of the tall boulders, raised the Colt. "It's over," he said quietly. "Put the rifle down."

He saw the black-clad figure stiffen, stay motionless for a long minute, and then slowly turn to peer back at him. "The rifle, put it down," Fargo said again. He watched the black mask turn away, start to lower the rifle to the ground when, with unexpected quickness, the black figure hurtled sideways, diving behind the boulder. Fargo's finger tightened on the trigger, but the figure had disappeared from sight. Fargo dropped down to the flat rock, peered around the stones. The slave hunter had vanished and Fargo stared down the narrow passageway. In quick, crouched strides, he followed down the passage, reached the end where it bisected another narrow defile. He bent his powerful legs, leaped across the intersection of the passages, expected to hear the sound of the rifle thundering in the narrow passages. But there was only silence and he spun, peered out into the bisecting passage. Only the empty path and the stone walls met his eyes.

He moved through the passage, halted, listening, heard nothing, and went forward again. But the silence was not his only companion among the rocks, he knew. The black-clad figure was somewhere near. He could feel it in the way the hair on the back of his arms grew stiff, in the knots inside his stomach, the animal sensitivity to danger that was a part of him. He moved down another passageway that opened at right angles, the sides lower than the one he'd just left. His eyes moved along the tops of the rocks, alert to a shadow, a movement, a jutting spot that could serve as a hiding place. The passage came to an end, opening onto a small sunlit area of low stone clusters. He halted and let his eyes sweep the scene, moving back and forth across the mounds of stones that dotted the flat rock. He was about to step into the clear when he froze, his eyes fixed on a place at the edge of a near cluster of rocks. The very tip of a black boot barely protruded from behind the edge of the stones.

Fargo's mouth drew into a thin line and he pressed his back against the wall of the rocks, began to edge out into the clear, moving to circle the stones. When he reached the back of the mound, he ducked, gathered the steel in his powerful leg muscles, and sprang forward. The leap carried him past the mound of stones to land behind the waiting masked figure.

"Freeze," he barked as he landed in a half-crouch, and he felt the oath come to his lips, hang there as he stared at the single boot placed at the edge of the stones, the tip of the toe protruding. He straightened slowly, his lips biting down onto each other, and he turned with equal slowness, grimly aware of what he would find. He faced the rifle barrel resting over the top of another cluster of nearby stones. It was aimed directly at his chest, and behind it, the black mask peered down the sights.

Fargo nodded and his thin smile held a rueful admiration. "The boot was a nice move," he said. The figure made no reply and Fargo stared at the unmoving rifle barrel for a moment, returned his eyes to the masked figure. "You can take the mask off," he said. The figure didn't move. Fargo's voice grew softer, almost sad. "Take the mask off, Janet," he said, and he saw the black-clad figure stiffen. Slowly one hand rose, pulled the mask away, and Fargo enjoyed the complete astonishment that was mirrored in the china-blue eyes. "You had me fooled," he said quietly. "Until yesterday."

The little frown came to touch her face. "Because of the fight with that whore?" she said.

He half-shrugged. "Yes, but that was only part of it. Something else suddenly fitted," Fargo said, uttered a wry half-laugh. "Something Sam Tracy said to me," he finished. Her frown deepened and she waited, her eyes boring into him. "He said the slave hunter was some-

148

body who took it all very personal," Fargo said, fell silent, and the china-blue eyes stared back. " 'Nobody takes anything that's mine. Nobody takes anything away from me,' " Fargo echoed softly. "When you said that, it all came together with what Sam Tracy had said. Suddenly it was all there, all fitting. Even the little things fell into place."

"Such as?" she snapped.

"Why you despised the men in your circle and their association. I thought it was a sign that you didn't agree with what they stood for, that you felt differently about all of it. But it was because they weren't doing enough to suit you."

Her eyes grew darker. "That's right, inept, useless windbags, all of them, including my own brother. Those damn free-staters taking away what belonged to us, slaves getting the idea they can just run away and all there's to be done amounts to a lot of hand-wringing and talk."

"So you decided to do something," Fargo said.

"Yes, dammit, something that would put a stop to all this runaway business," she snapped. "Once and for all."

" 'Nobody takes anything that's mine,' " he echoed again softly.

She glowered at him over the rifle barrel.

"That hunting-up-new-business routine let you move around freely, but it was really all your idea, wasn't it?" Fargo half-smiled. "You just gave it to Dean and let him think it was his, and then you saw to it that he ran with it. The perfect cover and Dean the perfect front man. He went through all the motions you called and didn't even realize it himself. Neither did your father." Fargo watched the china-blue eyes bore into him. "You had every piece in place. When I happened by, you just added a few touches to make me a part of your masquerade. I figured I might be being used. I was in the right church

149

but the wrong pew. I just didn't figure it was you. You played it all perfectly."

"I didn't playact with you, Fargo. I meant everything," she protested at once. "You know that. You've got to know it."

"I suppose I do," Fargo allowed.

"All I wanted was for you to stay out of it," she said.

"And remember," he added softly.

"Yes, remember and come back one day," she said. "I still want that, Fargo. That's all I want." She lowered the rifle a fraction and he saw the pleading slide into her eyes. "Get your horse, ride away from here. Ride until the remembering makes you come back to me. Please, Fargo."

He studied her with narrowed eyes. "You'd do that, let me ride off with what I know?" he questioned.

"Just say you'll do it. I'd take your word, Fargo, always," she answered.

He turned the question inside himself before putting it into words, his eyes sharp on her. "What happens to Joseph Todd?" he asked slowly.

He caught the tiny lines that came to touch the corners of her mouth, pulling them down ever so slightly. "Forget about Joseph Todd, Fargo. It's not your problem. It never was. Just ride out of here and forget about all of it, please, Fargo," she said, and inside himself he felt the harsh heaviness settle like a grim cloak. He had hoped for a different answer, even as he was all but certain it was an empty hope.

The deep sigh stayed inside him. Her reply had shattered that sliver of hope, an answer that said nothing and everything. It was not just her convictions that burned inside her. Beneath the spun-sugar exterior he had first seen there lay a knife-sharp twist of character, a possessiveness that went beyond the normal. Or perhaps in the world she had always known, it was all too normal, he reflected. But convictions and inner character had turned her from an owner of men to a hunter of men, and there was no changing either now. The arguments, the fine-sounding words, the principles, they were all turned into bitter hate, unyielding, unforgiving causes.

"Fargo," he heard her voice cut into his thoughts. "Please go. Ride out of here." He shook his head slowly, sadly. "Why, dammit?" she flared.

"Promises," he answered.

"To a runaway slave?" she flung back disdainfully.

"Yes, and to myself," he said. He watched her mouth start to grow tight. The lips that had been so soft, so wanting, so full of pleasure, became a thin, harsh mockery of themselves.

"Damn you, Fargo," she hissed. "Why can't you ever listen?" He didn't answer. "Turn around," she ordered.

He met the fury in the china-blue eyes. "Can't you look at me and do it?" he asked.

"Turn around!" she half-shouted. He slowly turned from her, looked down at Boulder Road below, his back to her. "Damn you, Fargo, damn you," she bit out, and he heard the catch in her voice and he caught another sound, the soft rush of air being cleaved. She was bringing the rifle barrel down to smash against his head. He pulled his head to one side and the rifle came down alongside his temple, sharp, scraping pain, but he'd escaped the unconsciousness the full force of the blow would have brought. He spun, got his hand on the rifle barrel. "No, damn you," he heard her gasp. She slashed at him with her nails, but he ducked away, yanked hard, and wrested the gun from her hands.

He flung it a dozen yards as she flew at him, nails trying to rake his face, rage in her round face. "Goddamn you, Fargo, it's not your fight, damn you," she screamed.

He blocked her clawing hands, grabbed her, twisted

one arm, and she yelled in pain as he flung her to the ground.

"Stop it," he barked as she rolled to face him. "Stop it and listen to me." He stepped toward her and she shot out one leg, kicked him in the ankle, and the moment of pain made him half stumble. She sprang up at him instantly and this time he felt her nails rake across the already scraped side of his temple. He swore, swung his shoulder in a half-circle, sent her sprawling backward. "Stop it, all of it. No more, dammit, it's finished," he yelled at her as she picked herself up. He saw her move toward him again, her black-clad figure coming in more carefully this time. "I don't want to hurt you. I just want you to stop," he said, but saw the cold, insensate fury in her eyes. She feinted, stepped sideways, sprang from the other direction. He caught her arm, pulled downward, and brought her tight against him, grabbed the short blond hair with his other hand, and yanked her head back, and she cried out with the pain. "Will you stop, dammit. Stop it right now," he yelled, shook her head back and forth.

Held tight against him, she couldn't bring her hands up above his waist, but suddenly he felt the pull on the Colt. "Shit," he swore as he let go of her, grabbed at his hip. But she had the gun out of its holster, bringing it up to his abdomen. He half-spun, heard the shot, and felt it tear through the front of his shirt as he got one hand on the barrel of the pistol. He pushed the gun away from him as she fired again, and he heard the sharp, inward gasp of her breath. Her arm went limp against his and he pulled the Colt from her hand to see her stagger back. His eyes saw the ragged hole in the chest of the black jacket and his arms reached out to catch her as she slumped forward.

"Hell and damn," he swore, and now the catch was in his voice as he lowered her to the ground. He tore the black jacket open to stare down at the red stain that had begun to form, seeping from between the two high, round alabaster breasts. It trickled over the side of each breast in an almost identical pattern, as if an unseen hand were drawing a design. Perhaps it was, Fargo thought bitterly. The china-blue eyes opened, focused on him. Her lips moved, formed words that were hardly more than whispered sounds.

"Too late, everything too late," she said.

"Damn, Janet, why didn't you listen to me?" he asked, and heard the terrible bitterness in his voice.

She lifted one hand to his cheek. "Should have," she murmured. A little smile came to her, full of sad satisfaction. "You'll be remembering, though," she said. "I know it."

He nodded. "Yes, I'll be remembering," he said.

"How it was with us," she whispered.

"How it was," he said.

The little pleased smile stayed as she closed her eyes. He bent down and kissed her good night.

8

Fargo sat on the pinto in the center of Boulder Road and waited. Beside him, the black-clad figure lay across the saddle of the black stallion, and the big man's lean handsomeness was lined with grim bitterness.

He had risen to his feet atop the rock formation, silently cursing the way of the world. He'd scouted around until he found the black stallion, led the horse back, and gently put the soft, lifeless form over the saddle. He'd retrieved the pinto then, made his way back through the maze of passages until he reached the road below. He'd halted there and now he waited for the wagon. He heard the sound of it and the riders before it came into view, moving full out, two riders on each side. He saw Amity inside, sitting beside Joseph, a rifle in her hands. She half-rose as the wagon reined to a dust-scattering halt and she stared at the black-clad figure, the short blond hair that lay draped across the saddle horn atop the black stallion. Amity's eyes turned to the big man on the pinto, shock and astonishment swimming in the hazel circles.

"The slave hunter's finished," Fargo said quietly.

The shock continued to drape Amity's face. "My God," she breathed. "How did you know?"

"I didn't, not till the very end," he said.

"You were right about it not being Henson," she said.

"Yes, goddammit, I was right," he said bitterly. He

touched the pinto's side with the heel of his foot and the horse started to move on. "You can ride on easy now," he said to Amity.

"Where are you going?" she asked, alarm in her voice.

"I'm taking her home," he said wearily.

"No, they'll kill you," Amity cried out.

"I don't think so," he answered, not looking back, moving the pinto forward, his hand holding the reins of the black horse. He knew she watched him go until he was out of sight down the road and he kept on in a slow walk until he neared the Thornbury land. He turned, moved toward the big white-columned house, still looking misplaced on the Kansas soil. He rode toward it, entered the front gate, slowly approached the portico. Figures appeared, stepping from hedges, toolsheds, some from the house. Most were Thornbury workers, bonded in slavery, a few rangehands mixed in. All stared at the black-clad figure draped over the black stallion and all knew what they saw before them. The legend of the slave hunter was a household story in every slave quarter in the territory. But there were no smiles, no shouts of jubilation. It wasn't just fear that held them silent, he knew, as he saw their expressionless faces stare at the short blond hair, the silent, round face.

Richard Thornbury came from the house first and Fargo watched the man's face drain of color until he seemed almost lifeless himself. Dean Thornbury stepped outside, frowning, his thin lips drawing back in a soundless cry. Both stared at the black-clad figure and there were no words of explanation needed for them, either. Richard Thornbury's voice broke the stillness, an anguished, hoarse cry. "Get her down," he said, and two rangehands stepped forward to help Dean lift the figure from the horse. "My little girl. Oh, my God, Janet, Janet," the old man cried out as he knelt beside the limp form, cradled her in his arms.

Fargo's glance went to Dean Thornbury, saw the man's fists clenching and unclenching, his body trembling. Disbelief and shock churned inside the man, anguish and rage. But the black-clad silent figure and the black stallion denied his disbelief, mute evidence of the final truth. As Fargo watched, Dean Thornbury turned his anguished face to him, lips pulled back, the single word hissed at him. "How?"

"She grabbed my Colt and we wrestled for it when it went off," Fargo said. "I didn't want it that way, believe it or not."

He turned the pinto, started to move away through the circle of silent, dark faces.

As he rode out of the gates he heard the agonized, hoarse shout, Dean Thornbury's voice. "Fargo, I'll kill you for this."

Fargo didn't turn, kept moving forward across the dry land, and turned onto the road where thin stands of oak and rocky mounds took turns in bordering the path. He didn't hurry, his intense face still carrying bitterness in it, and he wondered if the cry of pain and shock had been just that or more. The answer would be his soon enough, he knew, and hoped it would be the latter.

He'd just rounded a slow curve when he heard the sound of the horse galloping all out. He halted, slowly swung from the saddle, and left the pinto in clear sight at the side of the road. A terrible weariness inside him, he moved behind a clump of roadside brush beside a slab-faced rock, drew the Colt from its holster. Dean Thornbury rounded the curve, yanked his horse to a stop as he saw the pinto, and leaped from the saddle. The man had gotten a rifle from the house, Fargo saw as his figure leaped into the trees on the other side of the road.

Fargo called out, spacing his words. "I didn't want it that way. It's done, over. Let it be."

"You killed her, Fargo. I'm going to kill you," Dean

Thornbury shouted back. A rifle shot split the air and Fargo saw it ricochet from the flat-sided rock to his left.

"She was holding the gun. It just happened," Fargo said.

"It wouldn't have if you'd stayed out of it," the man shouted back. "You had to chase the slave hunter. You had to look out for that goddamn runaway."

Fargo felt the deep sigh escape his lips, Dean Thornbury's words truth without the larger truth, truth wearing blinders. "We do what we have to do," Fargo called out. "Janet understood that. Leave it that way."

"I'll kill you," Dean Thornbury shouted, and fired another blast from the rifle. The shot went over the Trailsman's head. Talk was useless, he realized, Dean Thornbury gripped in shock, rage, helpless pain, a hundred more churning emotions that made reason impossible.

Fargo half-rose, started to run through the brush, staying crouched over, making no effort to be quiet. He let himself step out onto the edge of the road for an instant. Two shots slammed into the dirt at his feet as he ducked into the brush. He kicked at the brush ahead and saw it move, half-turned as Dean Thornbury emerged from the trees, the rifle at his shoulder. He blasted off two more shots into the moving brush. Fargo took aim, fired, one shot. The rifle flew from Dean Thornbury's hands as he half-spun, cried out in pain, and clutched one hand to his shoulder as he fell.

Fargo was beside him in a half-dozen long-legged strides, kicking the rifle aside. The man looked up at him, one hand on his shoulder, pain and defeat in his eyes. The sound of another horse going full out came around the curve and Fargo looked up, waited, certain who rode the racing horse. He watched as the horse came into view, Richard Thornbury in the saddle, the

157

old man's face filled with fear. He reined up, his eyes on the figure on the ground.

"He'll live," Fargo said grimly. "After you get his shoulder fixed."

Richard Thornbury dismounted, knelt beside Dean, studied the pain-racked younger man. "All right, I'll get you home in a minute," Fargo heard the man murmur. He holstered the Colt, walked to the pinto, and saw Richard Thornbury rise, come toward him. The white hair framed a face that was heavy with grief, but in the man's eyes Fargo saw relief. He halted, one hand on the saddle horn, faced the man. "I thank you for leaving me a son," Richard Thornbury said. "You could have killed him. I know that."

Fargo nodded agreement. "It's over," he said simply.

The old man's eyes seemed to move to a distant place. "I never suspected, none of us did," he muttered. "Janet was always two people, one very soft and sweet, the other very forceful, very possessive."

"I know," Fargo said.

The patriarch glanced at his son on the road. "Dean has some of her headstrongness. Even when he calms down, he won't forget this," the man said.

"Maybe he'll get another chance at me," Fargo said, and saw Richard Thornbury's eyes meet his. "Another day, another place."

"Yes," the older man agreed, and his face was grave. "I think the time is not too far away. You'll be on the other side, won't you?"

Fargo shrugged. "I don't know. I might be someplace else far away. But I know one thing. It'll be a terrible time."

Richard Thornbury nodded slowly. "Yes, a terrible time," he echoed.

Fargo pulled himself onto the pinto and rode slowly down the road. He hadn't noticed till then, but the night was quickly sliding across the land. He rounded a curve and the horse and rider were there, waiting at the edge of the road. He met the hazel eyes in surprise. "I sent Joseph on with the others," she said. "There was no need for me to go now." She turned her horse alongside his. "Come home with me," she said.

He nodded. "I need a little time for forgetting," he said to her, and saw understanding in the hazel eyes. A tiny smile came to his lips. "Sleep beside me. Nothing more, just that," he said.

She picked up his smile. "You trusting it'll be nothing more?" she asked.

He let a soft laugh float into the new darkness. "Seems to me I've heard this conversation before," he said.

"How much time?" she asked.

"See me tomorrow night," he slid at her.

She gave him a sidelong glance. "You going to be expecting or wanting?" she asked.

"Expecting," he answered blandly.

"Liar," she said. He watched the way her long, pear-shaped breasts swayed gracefully as she rode and knew she was right.

LOOKING FORWARD

The following is the opening section
from the next novel in the exciting new
Trailsman series from Signet:

THE TRAILSMAN #11:
MONTANA MAIDEN

The high plains country called Montana,
not yet a territory of its own,
a wild land where men made their own rules
to live by ... or die by.

"You want to tell me what the hell this is all about?"

Skye Fargo asked the question as, his hands bound
behind him, he took in the four heavy-barreled guns leveled at him. He let his eyes go to the four men behind
the guns, their stubbled faces made of grim hardness.
The one directly in front of him, a short man with a
broad, aggressive face, answered impatiently.

"I told you, it's about screwing," he said.

Instantly Fargo's mind flew backward, searching the
past as he stared in disbelief at the man. "Hell, I can't
think of anybody who'd be this mad," he murmured.

"Not anything you did," the man said. "What you're
gonna do."

The frown dug deeper into Fargo's brow. "What the
hell does that mean?" he barked as he twisted his wrist
bonds, found them well tied.

"It means we're getting real good pay to bring you someplace," the man said.

"Someplace where?" Fargo asked.

"Someplace where you're going to screw," the man answered.

Fargo's stare was one of continued disbelief. "Why the goddamn guns? Why not just ask?" he pressed.

"Because you either screw this girl or you don't walk away alive," the man barked.

Fargo's nonplussed stare stayed on the man as only one thought spiraled in his mind, and he gave it voice. "This must be the ugliest goddamn girl west of the Mississippi," he murmured.

"I don't know, I never met her." The man shrugged, turned to one of the others. "Get his horse. We've got to get moving," he ordered.

Fargo leaned against the wall of what was clearly a small shack somewhere as one of the men left. The frown stayed deep on his forehead as he let his thoughts go back over the past twenty-four hours. He'd been set up, that much was all too clear, handpicked before he'd walked into the dance hall, perhaps before he'd even arrived here in Wheeltown. He held the thought for a moment, set it aside. He'd start at the beginning, when he'd arrived in Wheeltown yesterday morning.

He'd ridden trail for three Conestogas carrying all the worldly goods of a very large family who hoped they could build a new life here where the Yellowstone and Bighorn rivers joined. They had an uncle waiting for them here, only it turned out that the uncle had caught six Sioux arrows two months ago and he was only a name on a crude wooden cross now. Maybe dreamers and fools were always one and the same, Fargo recalled thinking. It was the kids he felt sorry for, their young lives laid out for the taking by those with more hope than sense. Of all the untamed places, the Montana country was it, made for only the very strong or the very lucky. But the thoughts were his and he took them along with him with his pay and went to find Harry McAteer.

Harry had a tanner's shop in Wheeltown and Fargo had written him nearly two months back telling him he'd be rolling in one day. Fargo recalled how Harry had exploded in his roaring way when he'd walked into the shop. It had been years since they had ridden trail together and it was a time for remembering, for celebrating, a time for strong bourbon and weak women and the dance hall had supplied both.

Fargo thought back of how he'd made a note to remember the name of the place, the White Squaw Saloon, and now he had another reason to remember it. Harry had given up a little after midnight, and telling the girl to wait, Fargo helped him to his room over the little tanning shop, dropped him onto the bed, and returned to the saloon. The girl was there, waiting, and he remembered her clearly despite all the bourbon. Edna, not the usual name for a dance-hall girl, and she wasn't the usual type, either, a washed-out blonde with a long, thin figure and smallish breasts that hardly peeked over the low neckline of the dress. But she had good legs, long and willow-wand smooth, and she'd had a distinctive, tinkly little-girl voice that made her easy to listen to, and she fitted comfortably into all the remembering he and Harry had done. She'd seen to it that their glasses were quickly filled but, hell, that was part of her job.

Thinking back, frowning at the effort, Fargo remembered how her eyes had seemed terribly wide when he returned, almost frightened. "Let's have one more and then go upstairs," she had said.

Fargo had quickly agreed and she'd fetched the two bourbons, set his before him. She was looking more attractive, he remembered, the long legs suddenly very desirable. He finished his drink in three quick draws and she led him upstairs to a big room with a big bed and very little else in it. She closed the door as he sank down on the bed, looked up at her. Again, her eyes seemed terribly round and uncertain. She'd put her hand to the top of her dress, fiddled with the snaps below the neckline.

"You all right, Edna?" Fargo remembered asking. She nodded as the top of the dress came open and he caught a glimpse of the smallish breasts, remembered thinking how they matched her tinkly little-girl voice. He recalled how he'd started to rise up on his elbows on the bed when suddenly Edna became a blur, a fuzzy, shapeless form. He shook his head and she came into focus again. "Too damn much bourbon," he'd muttered. He half-rose and the room started to spin. He shook his head again and the room straightened out. He stared at Edna and fright was unmistakable in her eyes.

"What's eating you?" He frowned, got to his feet, and suddenly he seemed to have no legs, fell back onto the bed. Edna's figure became a blur again and he shook his head back and forth like a terrier shaking water from itself. She came back into focus and he stared at her. "Goddamn," he'd muttered. "That last drink. You put something in it."

She only stared back at him and he saw the door fly open, the four men rush into the room. He rose and the room began spinning away again, but he brought up a swinging blow that cleared his head as he felt it land on the nearest jaw. He had the satisfaction of seeing the figure fly backward before the scene faded away as a gray curtain dropped over his eyes. He remembered reaching for his gun, his hand moving down, touching the handle of the big Colt. He was doing everything in slow motion, the curtain in front of him now a purple gray. He'd felt hands seizing him, remembered bringing up a tremendous uppercut, somehow with enough force in it to cause a shouted oath of pain.

The blow jarred his arm and head, and the curtain parted for a moment. The men were coming at him, all except one who was on one knee. "Son of a bitch," Fargo heard one say. As the purple-gray curtain began to slip over him again he threw another blow, his powerful shoulder muscles fully behind it, and he heard the sound of a figure falling. Head down, he pumped blows, swinging wildly, the purple-gray curtain closing off all vision.

Someone landed atop his back and he felt himself falling forward. His arm struck something, a leg, and he wrapped his arms around it, pulled and twisted, heard the shout of pain, and then hands were yanking him away, rolling him over. He felt hardness, the floor, and what must have been a knee slamming into his back. The purple-gray curtain became thicker, heavier, drifted into blackness. He heard a voice, before he passed out, as if from a very far distance.

"Jesus, I'd hate to tangle with him when he's all himself," the voice said, and then the blackness had enveloped him and the world disappeared.

Fargo lifted his glance as the man returned to the little shack, his remembering over for the moment. "I've got the horses," the man said.

"Let's go," the short one with the broad, aggressive face said, and Fargo was led from the shack. He blinked at the bright sunlight, took a moment to adjust his eyes, and saw the pinto waiting. He was helped into the saddle, murmured a few soft words to the pinto, and watched the horse shake its head in greeting. "Helluva good-looking horse, that Ovaro," the broad-faced man said. He let a small, hard grin touch his lips. "Easy to spot, too," he added.

Fargo notched the remark in his mind. It fitted. He'd been picked. They'd known about him, how to find him

165

easily. The four men started to ride, two in front, one on each side of him, one holding the reins of the pinto. Fargo tried the wrist ropes again, tightened his hand muscles, but the ropes stayed secure, no give at all in the knots. He let his eyes scan the terrain. It was lush, fertile land, this Montana country, as full of beauty as it was danger, a wild land of mountain and valley, high plain and heavy tree cover. He glanced back at the little shack where they'd taken him from the saloon. It sat in a clearing, a thin pathway leading south from the door, through a thick stand of hawthorns, and he imprinted the terrain in his mind.

The men moved downward into a shallow valley, through country heavy with oak and hawthorn, birch, elm, and blue spruce, the thick bromegrass soft as a feather pillow underfoot. They rode into the afternoon with only an occasional exchange of words between the four men, and finally the broad-faced one called a halt, reached into his pocket, and fished out a crude trail map. He studied it for a moment, pulled his horse to the left. "This way," he muttered, started down a slow slope.

"This sure as hell makes no damn sense," Fargo remarked, blurting out the words angrily. "Why me?" he thrust out.

The man peered at him, shrugged. "Beats me," he said. "Maybe you've got something nobody else has."

"That all you're going to say?" Fargo pushed at him.

"I told you, we're just hired to bring you along," the man said.

"Who hired you?" Fargo asked.

"A friend of hers," the man said.

Fargo lapsed into silence and the frown touched his forehead again. It just didn't make sense. A girl who needed or wanted that bad could get it without any trouble, even an ugly one. Unless she was so damn ugly nobody'd touch her. Fargo made a face. It was possible, but it somehow didn't set right. Hell, no woman was *that* ugly. At least, he hoped not. The other question circled again. Why him? Why not someone else? He half-smiled, allowed himself a wry thought. He had something of a reputation and he'd never had an unsatisfied customer, but he wasn't conceited enough to accept that answer. He was still wrestling with the question when the house came into view, a small frame structure. The riders broke into a canter and Fargo felt his mouth tighten. He'd have at least one answer damn soon.

They reined up outside the house, the few windows with drawn curtains, the place silent. A man beckoned to Fargo and the Trailsman swung one leg over the saddle horn, slid to the ground. The broad-faced man took him by the arm, led him to the closed door, and knocked hard three times.

"He's here," the man called out.

There was no answer, no sound from inside the house, and Fargo frowned at the closed door. He was staring at it when it slowly swung open by itself. A room, made dim by the drawn curtains, came into view beyond the partly open door. "Inside," the broad-faced man said, helped him with a push in the small of his back.

Fargo stepped into the room and the man drew the door closed behind him. The Trailsman's eyes moved around the sparsely furnished room, a few chairs and a table, nothing more, and then he heard the sound, soft footsteps. His eyes went to the doorway of an adjoining room.

His hands behind his back, Fargo stepped forward, stared at the doorway. The figure came into view and Fargo found himself staring at one of the most beautiful girls he had ever seen.

"I'll be damned," he swore softly.

JOIN THE <u>TRAILSMAN</u> READER'S PANEL
AND PREVIEW NEW BOOKS

If you're a reader of <u>TRAILSMAN</u>, New American Library wants to bring you more of the type of books you enjoy. For this reason we're asking you to join <u>TRAILSMAN</u> Reader's Panel, to preview new books, so we can learn more about your reading tastes.

Please fill out and mail today. Your comments are appreciated.

1. The title of the last paperback book I bought was: _____

2. How many paperback books have you bought for yourself in the last six months?
☐ 1 to 3   ☐ 4 to 6   ☐ 10 to 20   ☐ 21 or more

3. What other paperback fiction have you read in the past six months? Please list titles: _____
_____
_____
_____

4. I usually buy my books at: (Check One or more)
☐ Book Store   ☐ Newsstand   ☐ Discount Store
☐ Supermarket   ☐ Drug Store   ☐ Department Store
☐ Other (Please specify) _____

5. I listen to radio regularly: (Check One)   ☐ Yes   ☐ No
My favorite station is: _____
I usually listen to radio (Circle One or more)   On way to work /
During the day / Coming home from work / In the evening

6. I read magazines regularly: (Check One)   ☐ Yes   ☐ No
My favorite magazine is: _____

7. I read a newspaper regularly: (Check One)   ☐ Yes   ☐ No
My favorite newspaper is: _____
My favorite section of the newspaper is: _____

For our records, we need this information from all our Reader's Panel Members.
NAME: _____
ADDRESS: _____ ZIP _____
TELEPHONE: Area Code ( ) Number _____

8. (Check One)   ☐ Male   ☐ Female

9. Age (Check One)   ☐ 17 and under   ☐ 18 to 34
☐ 35 to 49   ☐ 50 to 64   ☐ 65 and over

10. Education (Check One)
☐ Now in high school   ☐ Graduated high school
☐ Now in college   ☐ Completed some college
☐ Graduated college

As our special thanks to all members of our Reader's Panel, we'll send a free gift of special interest to readers of <u>THE TRAILSMAN</u>.

Thank you. Please mail this in today.

NEW AMERICAN LIBRARY
PROMOTION DEPARTMENT
1633 BROADWAY
NEW YORK, NY 10019